THE SECOND LIFE OF
EVERLY BECK

THE SECOND LIFE OF EVERLY BECK

THE TETHERED SOUL SERIES, BOOK 2

LAURA C. REDEN

The Second Life of Everly Beck:

The Tethered Soul Series, Book 2

Copyright © 2021 by Laura C. Reden

Ebook: ISBN 978-1-954587-05-2

Paperback: ISBN 978-1-954587-18-2

Hardback: ISBN 978-1-954587-06-9

Dyslexic Edition: ISBN: 978-1-954587-02-1

Edited by Maxwell Anderson

Cover designed by Laura C. Reden

Cover Images:

© Adobe Stock / alexlibris

© Adobe Stock / krstrbrt

© Adobe Stock / Kevin Carden

© Adobe Stock / Stephen

© Adobe Stock / donfiore

CONTENTS

THE SECOND LIFE OF
EVERLY BECK

CHAPTER 1

It was the fourteenth time I died, yet the first I wanted to live. Love will do that to you. The fear of losing Beck was far greater than anything I had ever experienced before. It was too soon. I was promised months longer—possibly a year. The wreckage stole everything from me. I didn't know it was an option for her to follow me. I'd never turned a mortal soul into a tethered one before. But that's how much I loved her. Enough to not let go, in sickness and in death. I meant it when I said, *forever*.

As a kid, my memory was clouded, leaving me with major gaps in my timeline. To put it simply, it was the best part. The ignorance. It truly was bliss. Though, for every gift that youth offered, there were drawbacks. Mine was that I had a secret to keep. In all honesty, it was a curse. An isolating burden that would cause me to squander my talents. To be seen but not noticed. If I had opened my mouth freely, I would no longer be "gifted," I'd be a "prodigy," and that was the line I drew between being normal and being something else entirely. A Tethered Soul was a tortured soul.

As a young boy that'd been around the block a dozen times or more, I mostly lived in the present. Being young was the best part of it all. No responsibilities. No backache, stiff knees, or dilapidated vision. I was damn near invincible. Or at least, that's what it seemed like. But unlike every other childhood I'd lived before, this one showed great promise when a little towheaded girl moved in across the street.

This is the story of my second life with Everly Beck.

Beck had survived death. I'd never been more sure of anything in my life. That's why I found myself in an underground gambling ring making dirty money; I had someone to provide for. Somewhere over the horizon, I had a wife, and I wanted to give her the world. There were, however, a few tasks that needed completion first, and I'd been working through them tirelessly. First, I had a standing appointment to see Clouse Charles, assuming he was still alive. Either way, at 3:00 PM, in the basement of a back-alley bar in the most dangerous part of Stills, I'd be handing over a large sum of cash for something much more valuable to me. It wasn't the first time I'd rubbed elbows with men such as these. Feral, savage beasts. Each with an outstanding criminal record. Because when you've been around as long as I have, it's hard to keep finances above board.

I was winning amongst the testosterone and cigar smoke when a leggy redhead placed my drink on the table with a wink. I'd seen that face before—the one that begged for a reason to run away and start anew. I smiled at her, taking in the invitation. She was a pure heart, much better than this place called for. I briefly imagined how I could turn her life around. How her troubled blue eyes could shift in the light of day. I could save her from this life. I wanted to. But I couldn't save them all, and my heart had already been given away. She wasn't Beck, and no matter how I pretended, none of them were. I took a sip of my drink, focusing on the game again, and when it was my turn to lay cards down, I did carefully. I collected my chips at the protest of the beast at the round table.

The men shouted, throwing their hands in the air. One went as far as repositioning his gun on the table to point in my direction. I won the pot when it mattered most, but lost often enough to make it believable. This wasn't the kind of place where you wanted to be taken for an outsider. All of these men had short lives ahead of them, and none were bright. Their energy didn't lift into the air; it sank like a heavy poisonous gas that cloaked the ground in darkness.

I'd been inhaling cigar smoke for four hours in anticipation of my meeting, but I couldn't keep this up much longer. My welcome had worn. When my 3:00 showed up, I withdrew from the game and cashed out with the bartender. I patted Clouse on the back and pretended not to notice as he marveled at my stature the way he had twenty-some years ago. "Still drinking scotch?" I asked. He smiled, and his silver-flecked beard split in two as he laughed out loud. "Two," I said to the bartender, tipping him a chip from my winnings.

"Easton Green, you never change, son. I wouldn't

believe it if I hadn't seen it with my own eyes." His voice trailed off.

"You're looking well yourself. Do you have the key?" I asked, sliding him his drink.

"Do you have my cut?"

I didn't mess around. I trusted Clouse. He'd been part of a long line of men that dealt with Tethered Souls and other powerful, dangerous beings. Keeping their safe deposit box keys for gaps of time that made little sense to anyone, printing fake IDs and passports when needed. They never asked questions, and they always delivered. All secrets were safe for a cost. I was happy to pay. I slid him a briefcase, and he handed me a single gold key.

"Will you be back, Mr. Green?" Clouse said, peeking into the briefcase, satisfied.

"Always. Keep my account open," I said, throwing back my shot and patting him on the back. It would be the last time he saw me, given his age, but there would always be someone on the other line ready to answer the call of a Tethered Soul—assuming the price was right. I left without turning back, and my stomach twisted when I heard shuffling in my wake. My hair stood on end when a gunshot echoed up the stairwell. The blood drained from my face as I took two stairs at a time. I had seen so much crime that sometimes I could convince myself to turn a blind eye. It was easy to do when the men had black mist pooled at their feet, but as I walked down the alley, I struggled to dismiss the leggy redhead who deserved better. It wasn't my world, however, and I had no choice but to keep on walking.

I proceeded to the bank and withdrew more than enough to get me started with a new life. Over the years, I'd dump my overflow into the account before making my exit into the next life. It was the only nest egg I had, and sometimes, I didn't even have that. I'm not sure what Clouse's men thought Tethered Souls were, but by the service they provided, I had to imagine they thought we were vampires or werewolves. Something that could not only siphon their blood and tear their flesh, but would do so at the drop of a hat. If they had only known we were like them, lonely and broken, caged birds unable to fly . . . well, I don't think they would work for us at all. And my guess was, that's the precise reason Tethered Souls said nothing about who or what they really were to anyone.

I moved swiftly down the streets. The cold air nipping at my nose, and my breath visible. I threw the tail of my scarf over my shoulder and hailed a taxi. The second task at hand was finding an engagement ring. What I dreamed of giving Beck was her original ring, but I knew it was either six feet deep in the Clover Cemetery or her parents had it locked away in a keepsake box amongst her belongings. I considered this when I thought about how meaningful it would be to give her the same ring, but I wasn't about to break into her parents' house looking for it. As tempting as that may be, I needed a replacement.

Doorbells jingled above my head as I walked into a jewelry store. The air was warm and stale. A security guard stood at the door with his arms folded across his chest and a gaze that could deter even the stealthiest of thieves. "Can I help you?" a man asked. His hair was slick and jet black.

"I'm looking for an engagement ring. Simple yet elegant."

The sales agent led me to a row of glamorous bands that gleamed under the encased lighting. My eyes wandered over all the possibilities that could represent my eternal love. As I lost myself in the beauty of my bright future, I heard my eight-year-old adopted brother call out in a memory that was anything but distant . . .

"Trampoline?" Tanner said, halfway out the door.

Becca and I knew there was no time like the present. We took off at a full sprint through her kitchen and out the back door. Her backyard was marvelous. They had a pool and a trampoline. I could almost feel the heat beaming down on me that sunny day. The towheaded girl crawled onto the trampoline and turned around to give me a hand. We were friends the second our hands met.

That day, the three of us jumped high enough to reach the sky. My heart pounded with excitement, and I laughed at the little girl's hair as it stood on end every time she fell. We didn't have to say anything to know we shared an undeniable bond. That was one advantage of being a Tethered Soul. I didn't like it so much when I was old, but then, I could live like that forever and be happy. That day, the day I met my neighbor, the three of us were as free as birds, and my soul soared with no limits.

We played every day that magical, sweltering summer. But it all ended when school started and my family moved across the country. Back then, I couldn't figure out why it felt like déjà vu the very moment I said goodbye to Becca. It hurt me in a way I could only understand when I was older.

Even though my memory hadn't yet bloomed, I knew I was losing a very special piece of myself that day.

The older I grew, the more I was convinced of two things. The first, was that Beck was alive, going on her second life. I didn't know how, but I could only imagine that my love was strong enough to pull her soul to mine, and somehow, she stayed behind with me instead of moving on. The second, was that for a brief moment in time, she used to be my neighbor. I felt the gravitational pull towards her when I was young, but now with the clarity of my memory in full force, I could see the synchronicities. The bright blond hair, the green eyes, her name. Becca Reed. It was so close to Beck, it was possible that her new parents named her after her real last name. I never asked.

"This one," I said. I chose a single diamond that sparkled with resounding hope. It looked just like the original had, and I couldn't wait to find Beck and slide it onto her finger. This time, we'd have a proper wedding. And this time, it really would be forever. The only obstacle standing in my way was the third and final task at hand; I had to find her. I'd searched for loved ones before. Scoured the earth for little brothers, past parents, favorite mentors, and one time, a dog. But I'd never searched for her—I'd never looked for another Tethered Soul. When I started with records of her adopted parents' names and a past partial address, nothing had turned up. As was the case with most adopted kids, her records were all marked confidential.

It was hard to remember, but if I recalled correctly, my

first few lives had been messy. Of course, nothing had been worse than the original, though. I was nearly six when I died, and until that day, I was nothing more than my father's whipping post. I tried to block it out, but lucky for me, my subconscious did that all on its own—something for which I was thankful for. But the lives that followed were dark and lonely until the rules of the game finally made sense to me. I needed to be there for Beck during this confusing time, because remembering the impossible can be an uphill battle. Especially if the ones you trust to confide in don't accept you for who you really are. And they don't. They never do. Everly was the only person I'd ever told that loved me just the same when all was said and done.

In an ever-changing world, I had always stayed the same, and I knew Beck would too. If I had to guess, she was somewhere out there, trying to get an education in graphic design. It was the one and only clue that I hadn't yet investigated. I hoped she would fall into my lap much like she did on the New River Bridge. Appear out of thin air. Her soul not tethered to earth, but to me. Our love like magnets, fate willing us together.

It didn't happen. Not yet, anyway.

I'd spent two years checking out the golden coast and watching every equestrian that galloped through the crashing waves. It was one of her bucket list items she'd yet to check off, and I somehow envisioned her there with a golden tan and a wild mustang beneath her. Eventually, I rented a home up north, hoping to run into her during a breath-taking display of the northern lights. It was there, underneath the sky's green glow, that I'd find her wrapped in a blanket in need of my warmth. When that, too, never came to fruition, I spent nearly a year crashing weddings while traveling across the country. But I wasn't about to give up. No, I was just getting started.

It hadn't occurred to me earlier that Beck might return home, and I expect that this is because my first life wasn't one I'd ever return to myself. When I tried to empathize with how Beck might feel, I knew I had to go to Clover. There was something about home that could draw a warm soul in, and I had hoped that would be the case with Beck and the small town in which she had grown up. When the plane touched down, I ordered a cab to take me straight to the bridge. The New River Bridge.

CHAPTER 2

I stared out the window of the taxi as memories slowly took hold. While most of the commercial space had developed over the years, the lush pines of the forest remained the same. My heart picked up pace as the New River Bridge approached, and I rubbed my clammy palms onto the knees of my jeans. "You can drop me off here, sir," I said.

"Here?" The cab driver asked.

"Yes, thank you." I handed the driver a twenty and hopped out of the cab with nothing but a backpack slung across one shoulder. I stepped onto the curb and marveled at the bridge and the rushing water below. The air was electric, and my skin buzzed with memory. Now, all I had to do was find her. Again and again and again. My never-ending story was finally taking shape. The only problem? Where was she?

My fingertips grasped the platinum band in my pocket, twirling it from side to side as I stood at the very place we met, *and died*. She wasn't here either. Not today anyway. I breathed in the electricity in the air and I could feel that I was closer here than I had ever come before. Her energy seemed to waft in the air and wrestle in the trees. My eyes grew large as I took in the genuine beauty of the river and the optimism that it stood for. It was beautiful here, despite the pain.

I ran my fingers over the engraved plaque that read, "In loving memory of Easton Green and Everly Beck." It was a lifetime ago, but it hurt like yesterday. I shook the image of Beck's searching eyes submerged in the icy water of New River—an image that plagued me. Nothing was worse than helplessness, and I felt its full wrath in the wreckage that stormy afternoon.

I shook the memory from my mind, replacing it with a happier one:

"Easton! Come on down!" Mom yelled from downstairs. She was an impatient woman.

I rolled my eyes and let out a sigh. "I'm coming!" I yelled. She wouldn't hear me if I didn't yell, and I laughed at the ridiculousness of it.

Tanner threw his pencil, standing in compliance, and I followed him downstairs. He and I were the same age and adopted the same month. Mom and Dad had gotten two of us to keep each other company—like dogs I'd always thought. I liked dogs, though, and I enjoyed having a brother. As far as having a sibling went, Tanner was a good one.

"The new neighbors moved in. We're going to greet

them and bring some cookies. Go wash your face, Tanner. You have marker all over!" Mom hissed.

I didn't want to meet the neighbors. I'd been watching them out my window for a week. They had a girl, seemingly my age. She wore too much pink. Tanner reappeared, the marker faded by ten percent, no more. Mom let out a sigh and ushered us out the door while she grumbled something unkind to our dad. Tanner and I snickered behind them.

The day was dreadfully hot, and the sun beat down on my back, making meeting the girl next door even more dreadful than it had to be. My brother and I took turns seeing who could shove each other harder before my dad interjected, swatting us from behind. Tanner gave one last groan before Mom rang the doorbell, holding her perfect plate of cookies. We appeared to be the perfect family, except none of us shared DNA, and nobody ever talked about it. I wasn't the only one with a secret.

A woman opened the door, still drying her hands on a dishtowel. The women exchanged pleasantries, and once the warm cookies were handed over, the lady invited us inside. As much as I had protested before, I was more than willing to step into the air conditioning. My family and I sat on the sofa, Tanner and I like perfect gentlemen when it mattered most. The neighbor called her daughter down to meet us.

"Becca, come meet the neighbors!" she called. I still remember my cheeks getting hot in anticipation. But everything changed when I saw her. It was like I had finally found something I didn't remember losing. I smiled, gripping the bridge's railing as I grounded myself in the present moment.

The low hum of a motor whizzed by, and I looked over my shoulder, though I shouldn't have. It was tricky being back in town just one life over. I had a good chance of running into someone I once knew, and since I looked identical, only a little younger, it was something that I had to be aware of. It had happened to me before, coming face to face with past loved ones—it frightens them. It's painful to see someone they once loved but had to close the door on so that they could move on with their life. I didn't want anyone from Beck's past to see me. I pulled the baseball cap down to shield my eyes.

I stood there for hours, willing her to find me. I watched the river run wild. Listened to the blackbirds crowing above as they searched for prey. I counted the cars that passed by: eight. All the while, I slouched with an empty heart and a fear that I couldn't see. If I had only known she was safe and happy, I could take the time needed to find her. But I knew nothing for certain, and it was draining.

People like to say it's a small world, but you only hear that when a coincidence occurs. In reality, far more people are missing their chances than getting them. And more opportunities are lost than found. I wouldn't allow Beck to be a lost opportunity, though. I was going to find her if it was the last thing I did. Luckily, I had a lot of time on my hands, making the probability of keeping my promise strong. I lingered on the bridge until sunset, unable to pull myself away from the feeling of being closer to Beck than I had been in years. When the sun dipped behind the mountains and the air dropped several degrees, I decided today wasn't the day. I'd begin again tomorrow with fresh eyes and enthusiasm.

I hitched a ride to a nearby hotel, only stopping when I saw the Red Brick Diner along the way. I asked the taxi to pull over and keep the meter running while I grabbed some dinner to go. It wasn't the Red Brick Diner anymore, though, as all things change over time. Now, "The Taste of Italy" glowed above the doors, and unlike the Red Brick's signboard, this place had all of its letters in fully working order. It had a fresh look too. After a moment of debate, I decided I would take the chance of being seen, though I hid under the bill of my hat the best I could.

I tugged at my collar, trying to hide the lines of my jaw as I walked into the pizza joint. You never know what will spark a memory in the minds of the mourning, and sometimes it's something so little that it can't be described at all.

The smell of freshly made bread comforted me, and my focus turned to the grumbling in my stomach and the watering in my mouth.

"Can I help you, sir?" It was a perfectly round lady with a chip on her shoulder. Sue.

Did she remember me? I took a step back and looked down at the ground.

"Well? Can I help you or not?" she said.

"I'd like to make a to-go order," I said, looking everywhere but into her eyes. A pinball machine rattled and chimed as two kids thrashed about, their entire world spinning because of two quarters and a red button. A boy riddled with acne on what appeared to be his first date. And a couple sitting across the room from him with shifty eyes. His parents?

"Well, what'd ya want? I'm no mind reader!" Sue barked.

I looked her in the eyes. She needed this more than I worried about getting recognized. "I'm sorry, you just have the most beautiful eyes! You probably hear it all the time." I shook my head and looked away, hoping that she was as easy to win over as she was years ago. The Hawaiian pizza looked phenomenal.

"Oh! You devil, you! Stop that!" Sue giggled like a schoolgirl. My heart sank for her. So grumpy. So unhappy. She just wanted to feel special. But she was so scared of rejection, she made everyone hate her before they ever got the chance to see her.

"I'm serious! You go home tonight and tell your man, he's a lucky one!" I said.

"Ohhh, well, believe it or not, there hasn't been one of them in a long while. But I have to say, if you weren't so young, I might've gone after you, you handsome devil!" Sue trailed her hand ever so slightly across one of her large breasts, even though she was well into her seventies and I was twenty. Her efforts made me chuckle, and a slight warmth spread across my face. Sue bounced with amusement.

"Well, I guess in another lifetime, huh?" I said.

"Guess so. What can I get for ya, dear? The pesto is really good tonight." Sue pointed to a picture on the wall.

"Pesto? OK, that sounds great, I'll take one to go,

please." It wasn't my favorite. But the girl needed a win, and I'd already committed to being in her corner.

I paid Sue with a nice tip and sat in a booth while I waited for my pizza. I watched the people go about their lives, and I wondered who they were and where'd they go. I wondered what kept their minds satiated when the daily grind wasn't enough. I had my guesses about all of them, but I looked for clues that would stand for evidence. It was when I was mid-evaluation of a businessman ordering dinner, that I saw a girl with blonde hair escape into the ladies' room. My stomach dropped at the cool ash tone of her locks. I jumped to my feet as adrenaline coursed through my veins.

Was this it? Had she come home, looking for me? For her parents? I scanned the room before moving booths to one a little closer to the women's restroom, where she could not escape without me seeing her face in full. As the seconds ticked by, my palms started to sweat and the beating of my heart echoed in my ears. What would I say to her? How would she react when she saw me? Would she still love me?

The ladies' room door swung open, and my breath caught in my lungs. But when she emerged, my breath let out freely in despair. She was just another face—just another almost. Her skin tone was light, and her lips a contrasted pink; she looked a lot like Beck, but no doubt it was a different soul.

"Green! Pizza for Green!" Sue called out, her voice booming over the chatter and arcade games. I got up, disappointed, and retrieved my pizza but not before I put on a cheerful face for the server that had worked well past her prime.

"Don't be a stranger!" Sue called.

I turned around and waved to her. The blond haired girl caught my eye as her boyfriend reeled to get her attention as she stared mindlessly at her phone. "Everly! Look at this!"

I stopped dead in my tracks, my feet unable to keep momentum. Could it be her? Was it possible I'd forgotten the face of my soulmate? I shook my head, dispelling the thought. I could never forget. Then I realized as I peered over to her table, the girl must be Beck's niece. I squinted my eyes shut, taking a split second to absorb the pain, and then I forced myself forward. Tightness closed around my chest as I came so close but not close at all.

By the time I arrived at the hotel and got situated in my room, my pizza was cold. I tossed the box on the table and grabbed a slice, sinking my teeth into the cheesy pesto. It wasn't half bad, though Hawaiian would have been much better. I threw myself on the stiff bed and landed with a thud. Nothing like a rock-hard mattress to pair with my cold dinner and lonely heart.

I pulled up directions to Beck's old college on my phone and wrote them down on a hotel notepad. It would be the first place I checked tomorrow morning. Once I exhausted my efforts in research, I turned on the TV. Four slices of pizza and two hundred channels later, I fell asleep with the lights on and my shoes still tied tight. Sometime in the middle of the night, I'd kick them off and climb under the covers, but it didn't matter; I would never have a good night's sleep on that mattress anyhow.

I woke with a jolt; the room lit with the sunrise. It was the same dream I'd been having for the past month. The one with the woolly mammoth sized twin boulders. I dodged one successfully, but the other was about to shake loose and there was nowhere for me to run. I hopped to my feet and shook off the dream. Already dressed for the day, I collected my things and checked out of my room. I would have grabbed a coffee in the breakfast bar, but I had an itch for Fresh Ground's coffee, and I hoped they were still open some twenty years later.

I threw my backpack into the taxi and clasped the driving directions tightly. I didn't need directions for Fresh Grounds, though. That was still locked into my memory. Staring out the window, I reminisced about all the local spots Beck and I had once frequented. Hunters still stood strong, though it had received a facelift at some point over the years.

When we pulled into the parking lot of Fresh Grounds, I was disappointed to find that the place had closed, but at least what had opened in its place was yet another coffee shop. The cab driver parked, and I walked into what was now Stanford's Coffee. The little coffee shop had the same library vibe as before. Perhaps even more vintage now than it used to be. A few people waited in line, and I busied myself examining the changes. The faces of the employees were different, though the average age remained the same; they all were young adults. The seating configuration was a little different too, as they had replaced the leather chairs with old, green suede sofas that were decorated with ornamental wooden feet. The books on the shelves were so old they were falling apart.

"Sir, can I help you?" a young lady called to me.

I took several strides forward, unaware of my surroundings and lost in memories.

"May I have a latte to go, please," I asked as I pulled my hat down around my eyes.

"Sure, that will be $3.99," the pixie cut barista said.

I frowned, took out my wallet, and handed her a five-dollar bill.

"Thank you. That will be right up," she said.

I placed my change in the tip jar and busied myself looking at the old book spines. The smell of a good book only intensified with age. I imagined what treasures they hid within. What wise, artful words were left behind though the authors themselves were no longer here to share their stories.

"Latte, to go!" the barista called out.

I picked up my coffee and headed straight for the cab. "Step on it, my friend," I said to the driver. As we got closer, the gentle tugging at my soul became increasingly urgent. I knew I was on the right path.

CHAPTER 3

$\mathcal{N}$orton University was breathtaking as I stared out my window. The institution was made of stately red brick and covered in old ivy. The lush green lawn stretched for what seemed like miles. Students everywhere. My eyes scanned the crowd, trying to find Beck, but there were too many to vet them all. I didn't know if I was in the right proximity or not. Still, I had to try.

I stepped out of the car, and the gravel crunched under my shoes. The spring air was crisp and full of promise. My eyes bounced from every ash blond head as I made my way through the courtyard. Small groups of students with books in hand gathered at the benches and leaned against various trees. I listened to the conversations as I passed—in one ear and out the other.

"Brian's a prick. Don't listen to him!"

"Did you see the latest episode of . . ."

"Sorry, I have to work tonight. But maybe I can . . ."

I took the stairs two at a time, eager to get inside. It didn't disappoint. High vaulted ceilings. Ornamental wooden staircase. The college was stunning. I could see why Beck had chosen it in the first place and why she might return. I walked the halls checking countless class names until most of the students had disappeared and the chatter quieted. When a tall slender woman wearing a name badge passed by, I thought I better ask for help.

"Excuse me? Can you point me toward graphic design?"

The lady slowed her rushed pace just long enough to answer my question. "Yes, you're going to want to head over to the west wing." She pointed vaguely as she spun back around and continued on her mission. As my luck would have it, I'd been wandering in the wrong direction.

Making my way across campus once more, my memory drifted back to the day Beck and I had pretended to wed as children. All I had to remember her by was the one photograph. We had been eight years old the day we got married. She made me wear her dad's dress coat and tie. She wore her mom's dress and sunglasses. Beck held her pet bunny—our witness—who was also dressed for the occasion. Her mom thought it was adorable and snapped a photograph. Printed two copies for us to keep. It had hung on my bulletin board back home. Every now and again, I'd take it down and wonder where she was and how I would find her. If it was truly her—and I knew it was—we'd have an eternity to find one another. But if I was lucky, I wouldn't have to wait that long.

I scanned the classroom plaques, which told me I had made it to the arts wing. I passed several classes where

Beck may have been, had she chosen the same career path as she did in her last life. I picked an introductory graphic design class to kick off my investigation. Slipping in the back of the class with little disruption, I took an open seat next to an older gentleman. My spirit lifted at the sight of people learning in all stages of their lives. Whoever said you can't teach an old dog new tricks was simply inept. The man smiled at me as I took my seat.

I placed my backpack on the ground. Unlike all the other students here, my backpack was filled with clothing, not books. My stomach wrenched with excitement at the thought that Beck could be sitting just a few rows over. Would she make a scene when she saw me? Scream? Drop her books and bound into my empty arms? Would I propose to her right then and there? *Should I?* Right here in front of everybody? I saw it then, myself on one knee, presenting her with the ring. She'd be cupping her mouth, stifling her squeals, and the students would be spellbound. The story would turn into gossip, changing along the grapevine until it was a different version altogether. It was kind of romantic in its own way.

I lost myself in the daydream. It wasn't until the gentleman next to me packed his stuff that I snapped back to reality. Faces were passing now, and I searched them one by one.

I spent my day on repeat until the school day was done and I'd marked off three classes and one lunch hour. Unless I wanted to come back every day of the week and sit through as many classes as I could, I would have to find a better way. I pondered the idea of hacking into the school's database and searching the attending student list and schedules. Unfortunately, in all my years, hacking was one of the few things I never studied.

I swung my backpack over my shoulders and started the long walk to the parking lot. My eyes searched the various faces as I questioned if my childhood neighbor had been Beck at all. I was young and impressionable. Had I made it all up to comfort me in a time of grief? Was I in love with my childhood neighbor, *and* the girl from my last life? I frowned at my fresh worry with distaste, and I rubbed my hand across a furrowed brow to erase my angst, though I still felt it in my chest. Surely, there wasn't two loves in my life. As I walked through the sea of bodies, I was transported back to the ridge of my dream, where the monstrous boulder had begun to rumble.

I sighed. I thought living a few hundred years with no purpose was hard, but nothing could be worse than finding your purpose and losing it. Now that I'd felt Beck's love, I couldn't go back to a life of solitude. My very existence clung to the hope that she was alive and waiting to be found. *"You found me."* Her voice still floated through my mind, clear as the day she had said it.

I located my ride and opened the trunk. As I threw my backpack inside, I caught only a split-second glance of the back of a head. Ash blond. Ducking into the passenger's side of a white truck. Frozen, I watched as the truck drove away. Before I knew any better, she was gone. What made that blond head any different from all the others? I hadn't even seen a face, yet somehow my sights were set on this girl and this girl alone. Could I rely on my wrenching stomach? Or my eyes that saw only the back of a girl? I couldn't. But something inside me was telling me I *should* listen to the pulling on my chest. Like an anchor set in my heart.

Even though I knew Beck would most likely not come to school every day of the week, I did. After leasing a new black BMW, I finally had a place to gather my belongings. It was my first step out of the transient life and into one with roots. Never being one for commitment, I yearned to have it all with Beck.

I brought a laptop, sat under a large oak tree with a vast view of the open courtyard, and busied myself in the stock market, buying and selling stocks until I was sick of making money. The sun made its way across the sky, and I remained still beneath it as I waited for her. I knew now that I didn't need to see the faces passing by, I only needed the tugging in my chest to become so strong I'd be forced to follow it. Two days is how long it took for that familiar feeling to resurface, but it might as well had been an eternity beneath the oak tree.

Nearly forty-eight hours after my first potential sighting of Beck, it happened again. My heart pounded, and my palms moistened. The smell of grass became overwhelming and the sun almost too bright to see. Tiny goosebumps stood to attention on my arms as if receiving the signal. Every sense I had was now sharper, as I knew my chance had arrived, and I couldn't miss it.

I searched for what I could not see but knew was close. A group of three blond girls walked by. In the far distance, I could see a figure similar to Beck's. A small frame positioned on the stairs. A face buried in a hoodie, reading a book. None of them were Beck. It was only when I started to doubt myself that I saw the white truck pull into the parking lot.

My posture straightened, and tree bark scraped into my back. Regardless of the distance between us and the small blurry figure that stepped out of the passenger's seat, I knew it was her. Like knowing wholeheartedly, I loved Everly Beck despite never having the time to confirm it. Like trusting yourself, even though time and again it had been proven that you shouldn't. I didn't have to see her face to know it was her, because I felt my heart stop in my chest. I sighed in relief, for I had finally found her. And then when my heart started to beat again, this time it was . . . stronger.

I swallowed the bile caused by unruly nerves and scrambled to my feet at once. My laptop fell to the tree roots below. My hand found its way into my pocket, and I slid the cool platinum ring onto the tip of my finger. I watched as Beck situated her backpack and adjusted her hair before a large brute of a man rounded the truck and slid his arm around her shoulders. My stomach tanked. Together, they walked onto campus, talking amongst themselves. Beck glowed a little differently than before.

My nervous fidgeting stopped, and my jaw slackened. The ring felt foreign and misplaced in my hand. A dull ache spread across my abdomen—as if I'd been hollowed from the inside out. I thought finding Beck was the only obstacle that stood between our happily ever after, but I was wrong. Ignorant. Like a young boy in love for the first time, I hadn't realized that there would be unforeseen obstructions. Boulders on a steep ridge.

I watched them walk through the courtyard in slow motion as they made their way to the grand staircase. Beck playfully shoved the guy, and he grabbed her back into his possession. The sun suddenly became too hot, even as the shade cast down upon me. I stared as Beck and her boyfriend disappeared into the college. There I remained, frozen in her wake. Unbelieving.

CHAPTER 4

It took longer than I'd like to admit before I was collected enough to sit down again. But when I did, I got to work, mentally putting the pieces of what I had known to be true back together again. I wrapped my head around the idea that I might have to watch Beck be torn between her current romance and her past one. I knew she would come back to me. It was fate—like simple math. But what I didn't know was the grey matter that blended the black and white together. I didn't know how long it would take for her to become mine again or how steep the road ahead might be. Either way, I was in it for the long run. Not because I was noble, but because I had no other choice.

Beck was the first thing in my many lives that made any sense. Her becoming tethered to live out her second, third, fourth chance with me by her side . . . that was nothing other than destiny knocking at our door. I had to see it through. And she did, too.

I remained under the shadows of the tree, waiting,

thinking. I wasn't entirely sure what had to be done, but I knew I had to see her again. I hoped that when she caught sight of me, it wouldn't matter that she had a boyfriend. Nothing would matter. Time would stop, and we would reunite. Start a new life unbound by time. I tried to convince myself that this was the only possibility. Because how could her boyfriend's love ever live up to what we had? It *couldn't.*

Before lunch rolled around, my eyes fell on Beck once more. I felt like a coward for not rushing up to her, but I couldn't move. The fear of being unloved froze me. An eternity of knowing love was right outside my grasp. Surely it would put the fear into anyone. Beck's boyfriend threw such a wrench into my ultimate plan that I didn't know how to proceed. It certainly wasn't with the ring in my pocket.

I watched Beck as a friend of hers approached. They talked for a bit before Beck set her bag on the ground and threw her hair up in a ponytail. She was even more beautiful than I remembered. And I could see that she had a long life ahead of her this time. The energy that surrounded her was strong and youthful. Somehow, her eyes found mine as she reached to pick up her bag. And for a moment, I felt it. We were back together. She and I like Bonnie and Clyde. My heart stitched back to a complete piece. A smile spread from my lips to my eyes.

But just as quickly as it happened, it unraveled at my feet, the stitches in my heart pulling apart all over again. She'd looked directly at me and then away. *Nothing* happened at all. Was it possible she didn't see me? I pried my eyes off of her blond locks and looked all around me. I was the only one in the general vicinity. Maybe her vision was blurry like mine? Maybe the thought of seeing me again was so far-fetched that she just dismissed it?

But when it happened again, I no longer knew what to think. My heart beat against my chest. She saw me alright. She'd even stolen a second glance before going back to class. Perhaps the life she had made for herself was preferable to the one she had shared with me. The one where she had died. I could see how I might remind her of terrible times. My face was the last thing she saw before drowning, and her eyes burrowed into mine with her last breath. All I could hope for now was that she didn't associate me with the grim end of her brief life and turn me into baggage. I was so much more. I *could* be so much more.

I stayed put all day except for one trip to the restroom that I could no longer ignore needing. I hurried back, sure I hadn't missed another sighting. A small sense of relief washed over me when Beck emerged from the exit doors and into the courtyard where I had squandered my days away. I clenched my jaw as her boyfriend found her hand and walked steadily by her side. I hid behind my sunglasses like a true yellow-belly. When Beck cocked her head behind her shoulder with the direct intention of finding my figure under the oak tree, I found the courage to lift my sunglasses and meet her gaze, eye to eye.

She was close enough this time I could see the grimace on her face. Her hair caught wind in slow motion and danced under the sunlight, trailing behind her. My heart ached, and I grabbed at my chest to feel the pounding under my palm. Ever so slowly, she turned her focus ahead, and before I knew it, she was driving away. Just as quickly as she had come, she had disappeared, taking my hope for our future with her.

I sat for a long while under the tree, unpacking my predicament. I was pretty sure she knew it was me, but she wasn't yet sure she wanted another lifetime by my side. It was worse than any circumstance I had come up with in my head. By the time I was nearly suffocated with self-doubt and pity, I took my remains back to the hotel for another sleepless night.

It was a long, lonely evening. Even more so than the nights before. I could imagine the rejection when she was finally forced to say it aloud. "I don't want a second chance with you." It hurt enough in my mind, and I wasn't sure what I'd do if those words ever spilled from her mouth. I'd die right then and there of a broken heart. But that's not even the sad part. The sad part would be when I was born again on the same day to grow up and feel the pain all over again.

I'd all but given up for the day. I'd had enough of myself and wanted nothing more than to quiet my mind. It was too cruel—in only the way that honesty could be. I undressed and noticed something that made my night even darker and more disheartening. The ring in my pocket was missing. I checked furiously through my four pockets several times over. I scoured the hotel floor, retracing my steps through the tiny room. It must have fallen out with my hope while I sat under the oak tree for hours upon hours.

Was it fate? Was life telling me that Beck was no longer mine? I imagined the diamond sparkling in the grass, and I wondered who would be the lucky person to find it. For a split second, I thought about driving back to the college with a flashlight. But enough was enough, and I had to know when to quit. It was late, and my soul was in a million pieces sprinkled throughout Clover. It was quitting time. At least for today.

I woke in a panic. Sweat-soaked sheets and a heaving chest. *The ring!*

I scrambled out of bed and grabbed my belongings. I raced to the college as quickly as I could. I didn't know which fear was greater, someone else finding the ring or it being consumed by a riding lawnmower. Either way, I had to find it . . . fast.

It was Friday, and from what I gathered, Beck only attended school on Tuesdays and Thursdays. I wouldn't see her for five more days. I was neither saddened nor discouraged; I was hopeful. I hoped that she would have clarity by the next time I saw her. I hoped that I would have had enough time to pick up the pieces of my heart before standing before her. Nobody wanted to be broken. And first impressions were everything. Well, second first impressions . . . but they were basically the same thing.

I had a hard time finding a parking spot, but when I did, I picked up speed across the lawn. The anxiety reached new levels when I saw two girls had taken up residency under the oak tree. No doubt they had found the ring. They probably had a long discussion this morning about whether they should turn it in or keep it. How in the world would I convince them it was mine?

The girls fell silent when I approached them, both staring at me questioningly. I did a quick assessment. They were of the intellectual type. Cute in their own right, but clearly not girls that were used to the attention of the opposite sex. I didn't want to come off too strong. My focus landed on the books between them. Bookworms. Some of my favorite people were the ones who loved to lose themselves in the pages of a good book. I'd done enough reading in my days to fit into most book club meetings without a misstep. I wiped my palms on my pants as their foreheads creased with confusion over my intentions.

Honesty. It wasn't the only way in, but it was the best. These girls could probably spot a fraud a mile away, and I was tired of acting.

"Hi." It started off rocky.

"Um, hi?" One girl looked to the other. She went for the prim and proper yet vintage vibe and had an apparent love for mustard yellow and other muted colors. Her friend pushed her glasses up the bridge of her nose and stared at me, waiting.

"Any chance you've seen an engagement ring in the grass? It dropped out of my pocket yesterday, right about here, where you're sitting."

The girls immediately began searching the grass. They'd not come upon it yet. I crouched down to examine the grass with them.

"Sorry, I haven't seen it."

I crawled around on my hands and knees until the girls were so uncomfortable, they abandoned their post. At first, I was excited to see if it had been beneath them, but there was no such luck. With the girls gone, it was clear I wasn't finding the ring. Someone else already had.

After nearly an hour of searching, I retreated to my car. Water-soaked knees and two empty pockets. I suppose I didn't need the ring, anyway. I had gone to bed last night hoping for a better day, but this morning was off to a terrible start, and the boulder had begun to roll down the mountain. I needed a coffee.

Stanford's Coffee was buzzing this morning. I stood in the back of a long line of caffeine-hungry consumers. My mind had finally fallen quiet, and I gazed off into the distance, thankful for the reprieve. Every few moments, I would awaken to take another step forward. But when the doorbells chimed, and the air shifted with familiarity, my mind perked alive once more. I relished the moment of wonder. I loved the feeling of familiarity. It was like nostalgia, and it never got old. A red box with a bow. Who was it? What was it? I didn't want to find out. I only wanted the feeling of hope to spread until my mind was bright and clear again. I took another step closer to the register.

The sound of a woman talking to her friend several customers back pinged. She was the source of the familiar feeling alright, but I couldn't place the voice. Clearly, it had changed with time, and it would take concentration to find the subtleties.

"I don't know. I need to talk to John. See what he thinks," the woman said.

I took my last step forward and greeted the barista at the cash register. I ordered a large coffee, black, and an egg sandwich. I gave her my cash and my name before turning around to meet the mystery voice. And when I did, I was pleasantly surprised.

Beck's old friend Lindsay was standing in line. Age had been kind to her, and she was a beautiful middle-aged woman. Her hair was a natural dirty blond and her blue eyes glistened with sadness. She and her friend wore pink nursing scrubs, but I didn't bother checking her ID card. I knew it was her without a shadow of a doubt.

It was a standing room only, so I found a place near Lindsay where I could wait for my coffee. I listened with my back to her.

"How long do you think you will be out of work?" asked the friend.

"I don't know, I'll try to get back as soon as I can," Lindsay said.

"Don't push it. We have more than enough staff to cover you, and you'll need rest to recover."

"I know, I know. That's what they say." Lindsay was clearly upset with her situation, and it disappointed me that she didn't have Beck to help ease her through whatever she was going through. "But four to six weeks is a really long time."

"I've heard the laparoscopic hysterectomy recovery is shorter, though. Jess had one, and she was moving around after a couple of weeks. Her major complaint was being tired—um, hi! I'll take a cappuccino to go, please. What do you want, hun?" the friend asked.

I didn't know what was going on with Lindsay, but I figured that with her job, whatever it was, at least she knew the right people to get the best help available. I only wished her blue eyes weren't so sad.

"Easton! Order for Easton!"

Startled, I took my order from the table. As I made my way out, I caught the eye of Lindsay, but this time they were anything but sad. It was worse. Her forehead lined with disbelief, and her mouth slightly parted. Fear struck my chest, and I cursed myself for not having worn my baseball hat. I pried my eyes from hers and headed out of the shop in a rushed gait. It hurt me to know that Lindsay was standing inside that coffee shop with a flood of emotions and memories, and it was all my fault. I should have been more careful.

CHAPTER 5

Tuesday had come, and I was up early to see Beck. I had convinced myself that I wouldn't let her get away as easily this time. I would approach her, no matter what fears ran wild in my head. I would complete this one simple task: talk to the girl. I breathed in the deep crisp air of the campus lawn and cloudless sky. Today was the day I'd find out where I stood. After five days of living with the questionable voice in my head, I was ready to meet my reality. It couldn't be worse than the irrevocable damage I had already done by drilling into my head.

I perched under the oak tree, hoping that Beck would look for me there. While I waited, I couldn't help myself from running my hand through the wet grass. No diamond in the rough today. I sipped my coffee and waited patiently, searching every student that crossed the campus. When the brisk morning air became warm and sultry, I knew Beck had arrived. I looked to the parking lot to see the white truck in search of parking. Of course, her boyfriend would be with her.

Beck's eyes met mine even before she made her way out of the parking lot. She was looking for me alright, but this time, her friends were too. There was something in the subtlety of her movement that held me still in my place. I wanted nothing more than to run up to her, but her eyes told me I shouldn't. I swallowed the lump in my throat and leaned against the tree again. Maybe lunch would be a better time to make good on my promise.

It was close to noon when Beck resurfaced. Her arms locked with a tall girl; her hair as dark as chocolate. They made their way to the vending machine. I closed my laptop and tucked it under my arm and made my way over. It was now or never, and I convinced myself that nothing could be worse than waiting another two days for my chance to talk to her. My heart thumped in my chest as I approached the vending machine.

"You have to come! Payton is coming!" Beck said to her friend.

I took a deep breath and stood behind them.

"Oh, go ahead. We're finished," Beck said and grabbed her friend's arm, squeezing it tight. Our eyes met briefly before she hid behind her friend.

"Thanks," I mumbled, fumbling with the dollar in my hand and the laptop under my arm. This wasn't how I envisioned our reunion going. Disappointment washed over me and I tried to act as naturally as possible, but I was no stranger. Her eyes returned to mine, flicking back and forth between me and her friend. I tried to carry on with my selection in the vending machine, but I feared I was much more awkward than that. Beck's stare was more prominent now, and her jaw hung slightly. She could no longer hide behind her friend—not with that expression hanging in the balance. I was right there in front of her, and she had to say something. Anything.

I wanted to kiss her. I wanted to take her in my arms and never let go. But I just stood there, trying to smooth out my dollar bill, afraid of everything that could rain down on me. I'd never been so afraid in all of my lives, because the truth was, this was the first time I had something to lose.

"Nolan is bringing James. You're not going to want to miss this one," Beck said before her attention fell back to me. "I'm sorry, do you need help?" she asked.

"OK." And just like that, I was back on the New River Bridge. Rain-soaked lashes and her beauty still crystal clear. It was like meeting her for the first time all over again. Innocent. Hopeful. Full of possibility.

Beck took the bill from my hand as if in slow motion, her hand nearly brushing mine, close enough for me to feel the warmth. Her sweet scent—coconut—almost bringing me to my knees. I was so hypnotized, I barely noticed the vacancy in her eyes; she didn't share the same nostalgia that I was swooning over. She couldn't feel the palpable bond pushing us together. She couldn't feel it.

"I know you," she said, her eyes still searching for the answer. The impossible answer that wouldn't make sense to anyone in their second life. And that was it. That's what had happened. She wasn't stuck trying to figure out if she wanted a second life with me. She was simply trying to figure out who I was.

I could say so much, but in that moment, all that came out was a simple, "Yes," and I don't even think it was fully audible. I hoped she could read between the lines. My eyes filled with so much depth that surely, she could read me like a book . . . if she would just look deep enough. Long enough.

She couldn't.

The silence stretched between us until I saw the slightest shift in her expression. Her mouth opened to speak, but no words came out. She slowly let her hand fall—a tree in the forest—until she was pointing directly at my chest. "Oh . . . my . . . god," Beck began.

My heart felt like it had been hit by a semi-truck. The impact of her remembering me was so poetic, so magical, so memorable. It was better than in my dreams. I couldn't pry my eyes off of her. *Go on, Beck. Say it. Say you've missed me. Say you love me.* "I," I started.

Like clockwork, as summoned by the Devil himself, along came her boyfriend and wrapped a possessive arm around her shoulder.

"Can I have some?" he asked as he grabbed the bag of skittles from her hand. Beck's eyes remained on me, and her boyfriend took notice of our undeniable connection. "What's up? You know this guy?" he asked, frowning at the intensity of the moment. Our bond was so strong, it was tangible.

Beck's eyes reluctantly pulled away to look at her boyfriend. "Yeah! You wouldn't believe it! But this used to be my neighbor when I was a kid!" Beck said, and they looked back at me for confirmation.

Neighbor? Just a neighbor? It was like a dagger to the back. I never saw it coming. I wanted to take her by the shoulders and remind her of the life we shared—the memories of champagne and grass stains, but everyone was staring, and now was not the time. I resisted the urge and nodded slowly, confirming that, yes, it was true–we used to be neighbors. I had the picture to prove it, and it was right there in my wallet.

"Holy shit! Easton?" Beck shook her head in disbelief. "I *knew* I recognized you! What are you doing here?" Beck's voice was loud and boisterous, and I could tell that this was no act.

"I'm a student . . . here," I said and immediately wished I hadn't. I committed to the lie either way.

"Oh my god! It's a small world," she said, her eyes bursting with wonder.

It wasn't small though. It was an immense and infinite world capable of the unthinkable. All kinds of inconceivable things she couldn't remember.

"It really is," I lied, taking in the distrust of her boyfriend. The moment settled, and I knew my time was closing in. I had to do something so that this wasn't the end. I needed a way into their inner circle. *Her* inner circle. "Actually, I just moved here. I don't know anyone, and it's really something to run into an old friend." The word friend caught in my throat as if it were laced with acid, and I coughed to help clear the distaste. "Maybe you could show me around sometime?"

Beck smiled and her eyes lit up like a clear night's sky, full of stars and promise. "Absolutely! Sorry, how rude of me. This is Brooklyn," Beck motioned to her friend who was patient and welcoming. "And this is Nolan," Beck raised her hand to her boyfriend, and he glared at me in return. His expression screamed territorial but there wasn't an ounce of insecurity. If I looked like him, like I belonged on the cover of a men's fitness magazine, I probably wouldn't feel threatened by me either. But little did he know that I already had Beck's heart.

"Hey, I'm Easton. Nice to meet you."

Beck and her friends turned away, but Beck nodded with her head for me to join them. I crammed the unspent dollar back into my jeans and joined Beck by her side as I clung to the idea that she had not introduced Nolan as her boyfriend. He felt it too, and I wondered if it was a misstep or an intentional withholding.

"So where are you living now, Easton?" Brooklyn asked. I liked her immediately, she was a kind, gentle soul.

"Clover." I watched Beck when I said it, looking for any sign that it meant something to her. If it did, she had one hell of a poker face.

"Oh, that's not too far!" Brooklyn nodded approvingly.

"You guys, Easton and I were *best friends* when we were kids! Do you remember my trampoline?" Beck leaned in with a wide smile.

Everyone took a seat at a nearby bench and spread their belongings across the table, taking up real estate. Beck set down a half-eaten bag of Skittles and a Diet Coke.

"I remember your trampoline and the countless days of

summer we spent in your backyard." *I remember marrying you. Not once but twice.*

Beck threw her head back and laughed. "Do you remember when my rabbit scratched your brother, and he flung her at you, and you fell into the pool?" She managed to choke this out between fits of laughter. Not a care in the world. Beck was no longer dying but thriving. It was a Beck I'd never known before—but wanted to.

"Yes, I remember drowning in your pool. You refused to save me!" I teased her. I knew how to swim, of course, but I pretended to sink to the bottom hoping she would jump in and rescue me. It scared her, though, and I regretted my decision when it was all said and done. The look in her eyes was one I wasn't expecting. I was sent home after that. The parents had a long talk with us about pool safety that night.

"I was . . . *terrified* of the water!" Beck admitted. And I knew why.

"You still are!" Nolan said.

"Hey! It's . . . unnatural. We're not meant to be underwater, OK?"

Brooklyn frowned. "You really need to get over that fear. It's super weird! What kid doesn't love the pool?"

Beck lifted her shoulders. Her eyes darted frantically. "I don't know! Me, I guess?"

I watched her intently and wondered if she had any memory at all of drowning. My heart broke for her. I imagined there were a lot of unanswered questions and inadequacies buried deep within her. I did the only thing I could think of at the moment, and I changed the subject.

"I remember we got married that summer."

The conversation quieted, and Beck bit her lip and smiled up at me. "I remember that too." Her voice was endearing. Brooklyn's eyebrow raised, and Nolan snatched the Skittles out of Beck's hand, eager to interrupt the memory.

"Yeah, well, maybe we'll get married in Sin City next weekend! My birthday gift to you," Nolan said before emptying the remaining candy into his mouth.

Beck elbowed him playfully, and Brooklyn made cooing sounds in the background.

I'd been so busy trying to locate Beck that I didn't realize my birthday was coming up. Since she and I died in the same accident, on the same day, we shared the same birthday as well. But birthdays were like any other day of the week to me. They stopped being special when you'd had so many of them.

"Hey," said Beck, patting my arm—"That means it's your twenty-first birthday too!" The group was taken aback by this anomaly, and Brooklyn raised her brows in question.

"Twenty-one!" I said as any first-timer would; with excitement.

"Hey, Becca, our class is starting in five. We should go," Brooklyn said. I loved Everly Beck with all my heart, but who was Becca Reed? And how would I get her to remember me? The girls gathered their belongings.

Lost in thought, I watched my heart walk away on the arm of her friend. What was life throwing at me now? When I thought losing my soulmate was the worst thing that could happen, then this? I find her, and she doesn't remember me? Was this a cruel joke? Was it even repairable?

"Dude!" Nolan snapped from the other side of the table. I'd forgotten he was still with me. I glanced at him. He held his hands out like I was supposed to know that Beck was taken and I wasn't allowed to stare.

I stole one last glimpse of her before complying. "Sorry, man. What class do you have next?"

The first thing I did when I got back to the hotel was start a hot shower to rinse away the stench of defeat. When I finally relaxed, I lingered, unable to pull myself away from the scalding water and steam that enveloped me. My eyes cut through the mist, and Beck's drowning eyes haunted me. The fear of losing her all over again built until my eyes burned with tears and my breath quickened. I wondered if it would have been easier if I hadn't known Beck's love at all—easier than looking into her eyes and seeing an empty, forgotten bond. Was Becca Reed only the shell of a girl I used to know? Used to love? I placed my palms against the cool shower tiles until the tears ran dry.

It was when I closed my eyes that night that I returned to the nightmare that had been plaguing me. The boulder rolled down the mountainside, picking up speed, and I had nowhere to run. When I tripped and fell flat onto my stomach, the boulder began to crush me.

CHAPTER 6

$\mathcal{I}$ didn't make it to campus until a little before Beck would be out for lunch on Thursday. Not because I hadn't tried. I did. I sat in my car at 7:00 AM. The motor running, my hands tight on the wheel. I just never made it past park. I like to think of myself as a strong, multi-faceted, capable guy. But no matter how much experience I'd had throughout time, I wasn't prepared for being in love with someone who looked at me like a stranger. Being forgotten was one of the most painful events I'd experienced. And that was saying a lot.

I had to win Beck's heart all over again. Honestly, I wasn't sure I could. Today, my highest hope was that she would take me on a tour around the campus. It was so insignificant, and yet, I wasn't even confident I could achieve it. A part of me didn't want to try.

My stomach was so sick by the time I finally saw Beck that it was difficult to look her in the eye. She seemed well, though—possibly happier than I'd ever seen her. I questioned if I would hold her back in this life. My specialty was being a beacon of light in the lives of the dark and fallen. Now that Beck was thriving, I wasn't sure that I had anything to offer her. I couldn't shake the thought of letting her live out her life and finding her in the next one.

"Are you alright? You seem kind of down," Beck said.

"Oh, no. I just didn't get much sleep. That's all."

"Oh, I'm sorry." She didn't buy it. The telltale sign was the ruffle of her brows.

"Hey, do you think you could give me a tour?" I asked with nothing left to lose. I was surprised when she said yes. It was enough to elevate my mood a notch or two. When I pushed off the bench and we put some distance between us and her friends, I felt even better. Beck and I alone, walking side by side. It was the small things. I had to believe that one of them might spark and later, catch fire.

Despite the cool spring air, Beck wore a white sundress. It looked amazing on her. It would have looked even better if her boyfriend's jacket hadn't been draped over her shoulders.

"Have you not walked around campus yet?" Beck asked.

"Um, no!"

"You must be busy. Do you have a full schedule?"

I'd not thought this far. "Oh, wait, no I've seen this wing. Let's check out the library? I've been dying to see it."

"Oh, yeah, OK." Beck nodded, and we changed course. "I still can't believe we ran into each other. And here, of all places. I mean, it's not like we grew up here or anything. It's *so* weird," Beck rambled.

"Like, it was predestined?" I asked with a smirk.

Beck looked at me and smiled. Her cheeks flushed pink. It was the first time I felt like I was talking to her. The old her.

"Yeah, you could say that," she said.

"Well, it couldn't have come at a better time, because, like I said, I just moved here, and I could really use a friend. I'm happy to have found you." I opened the door for Beck and briefly placed my hand on her back as she passed through.

"I'm glad to have my friend back too. Um, is there something else going on I should know about?"

I lowered my gaze to the lobby floor. We were inside the college now, and I needed to keep my voice down. "It's nothing. I just found out I was adopted, so . . .":

Beck gasped.

It was kind of a dishonorable move, but I was working from the ground up. Not only were the odds stacked against me, but her picturesque boyfriend was too. I knew she would empathize with the shock of finding out I was adopted, and maybe I'd be in the club again. The Beck and Easton Club of Tethered Souls. It had a nice ring to it.

"I'm so sorry. Your parents just told you?" Beck asked.

"Yeah, just recently. Right before I moved here."

"And your brother? Is he adopted too?" Beck opened the doors to the library. It was a beautiful sight. Massive and historic. I took a deep breath; I loved the smell of books.

"Um, yeah. Tanner was adopted too." I waited for her to confess her adoption.

"Shit. That must have really thrown you for a loop, huh? Are you going to find your real parents? I mean . . . biological? Sorry!" Beck scrunched her shoulders up to her ears with a pained look on her face. *Real parents.*

She really didn't remember me, or she would have remembered that I didn't have parents. She never would have faltered, calling parents "real," just because they shared your DNA. And apparently, she didn't know she was adopted either. How had she not known this about herself? Why hadn't her parents told her the truth yet? It would be hard for her when she came to realize the truth. I only wished she had found out about her family sooner. It probably would have made it easier to accept what she now was. Not to mention the fact that it would have made my job a little easier too.

"No, it's alright. Um, I don't think I'm going to look for them," I said while I ran my hands down the spines on the bookshelf. They weren't people I'd want to find, even if I had the opportunity.

"If you don't mind me asking, why wouldn't you?" Beck leaned against a wall of books.

It was a hard question to answer, even if it was a lie. "I don't think they were fit to be parents. They didn't want to be found, and I can respect that. I'm just happy they gave me a better chance than what they had to offer." Only the first part was true—that they weren't fit parents.

Beck nodded, her eyes falling on a student walking in our direction. Our private conversation became less intimate, and our connection faltered. She turned around and pulled a book off the shelf and paged through it while she waited for our privacy to return. My eyes burrowed into the back of her head, and I yearned for our connection to return.

"That's a good one. You would like it," I said, coming up behind her.

Beck's eyebrows raised. "You've read this one?"

"Yeah."

She smiled. "That's random."

"I've probably read most of these books," I said honestly.

"Oh wow. You're a big reader!"

It was my turn to smile back at her. "I've got a lot of time on my hands," I said. I wish she understood. But she just looked at me in question. After a moment, she grabbed a book from behind her without ever looking at it. "This one?"

I glanced at the cover. "Yes."

Beck stacked the book on top of the other and took off down the aisle. She paused near the end of the fiction aisle and grabbed a small green novella. "This one?"

I chuckled. "Yes. Though I don't think you'd like it as much as the other two in your hands," I said.

Beck's eyes slanted, "And what makes you think that? You don't even know me."

"Do you want to read about the Siege of Kazan?" I challenged her.

Beck's eyes quickly scanned the back of the book before she bit into her lip and looked back at me with large doe eyes. "No," she admitted.

I closed the distance between us. "Beck, you seem to

forget that I was your *best* friend. And at one point in time, I was even your husband."

Beck snorted. "Oh my god, Easton! That was like, a lifetime ago!"

"Precisely," I said. It took everything I had not to lean in and kiss her. I wondered how it would be received if I did. Right here in the library where fiction ended. "One lifetime ago is not enough to change who you are. I'm sure you've changed, Beck. I mean, I know you have, but I still know you to be the little girl you were at eight years old. And I still see my best friend when I look at you." I stopped myself from bleeding out right there amongst the books. The truth was, I saw so much more than that. But she wasn't ready to hear it. Not today, she wasn't.

Beck smiled, and her eyes glistened. She placed a hand on my shoulder and pulled me in for a hug. "God, I've missed you," she said. My heart dropped. I wanted to hear it over and over again.

God, I've missed you. It echoed in my head.

"And if you ever need to talk about your parents or anything, you can call me. OK?"

"OK. Like anything?"

Beck pulled away too soon and checked her watch. "Oh, shit! I'm *so* late!"

I pretended I too had somewhere to be. "Oh man, where'd the time go?" I looked around, shoving my hands in my pockets.

Beck shoved the books back into a random spot on the shelf, and I tried not to cringe at the disorder.

"Hey, a group of us are going to Sin City next weekend

to celebrate my birthday. And actually, it's your birthday too, so you should come!" Beck said as an afterthought.

Sin City? "Yeah! I'd love to!" It wasn't my scene, but I'd do anything to be by Beck's side.

"This is going to be so much fun! Let me get your number real quick, and I'll keep you updated," Beck said as she glanced behind her as if time itself was coming after her. We exchanged numbers in a hurry.

"I'll call you," Beck called out as she charged off to make the remaining bit of her class.

I smiled and nodded. "I'm looking forward to it!" I called back much too loudly for a library and reaped the consequence when someone shushed me.

I had woken up with the highest hope of getting a school tour out of Beck. A tiny fraction of time alone with her. What did I get? A lot more than that! A whole weekend with her . . . and her boyfriend. I pushed my back up against the bookshelf. Her boyfriend. What had I gotten myself into now?

When my questions went unanswered there in the library, I resolved to head out. I'd already fulfilled my purpose of coming to the college today, and since I wasn't actually a student at Norton University, it was time to be on my way. But not before putting those three books back in their rightful places. I wouldn't allow Beck to sin by accident.

It's funny how an instant can change a perspective. One moment in the library. One look of curiosity. It was enough to set the hook, and I'd be there for Beck whether she wanted me as a friend or something more. At this point, I'm not sure she could get rid of me if she tried.

I'd need a house if I was staying long-term, and from the looks of Beck's schooling and friend base, I would be here awhile. There were a few options, but nothing exciting. Nothing in Clover was. The options I had available to me when I moved to Clover previously—to develop a relationship with Clyde—were slim to none. I chose the best house, but it still needed work, and while I had the time, I found myself living with the dysfunction instead of fixing it. I knew that would be the case for my next house as well, and I'd have to choose wisely if I ever thought Beck would move in with me.

I settled into the hotel for the night, anxiously awaiting Beck's promised call. Time moved beyond slowly, and I busied myself looking for real estate nearby. When the hunt bore no fruit, I watched a movie. And then, another. By the time 9:00 came, I couldn't wait any longer. The phone-checking had become impulsive, and I questioned why I hadn't called her myself. She was probably waiting for me to call, like I was waiting on her. Without any more thought, I picked up my phone for the umpteenth time and dialed her number. Was it too late? Would she answer? I pushed it all aside the moment I heard her voice.

"Easton Green. You know, I still can't believe that our paths have crossed for a second time."

My stomach wrenched at the sound of her voice. "I'm glad they have," I said.

"Um, about Sin City . . . now that you've had time to think about it, did you still want to go?" Beck sounded off, regretful perhaps, and I knew why. Though I didn't want to admit it to myself.

"Yeah! I can't wait. I'm . . . I'm looking forward to meeting some new *friends*." My eyes dropped to my lap and moved across the bedsheets in defeat.

"Great! I'll send you our flight information, and the hotel reservation, and you can book your stay. It's going to be so much fun!"

"Cool!" I cringed.

"OK. I'll, um . . . , I'll see you next weekend then," Beck said in a much lighter and more confident tone.

"OK. Bye."

"Bye!"

I wished I hadn't called. The realization pulled me down like a cinder block tied to my ankle. Beck didn't like me. It was as simple as that. The subtle drop in her tone when I made an advance was obvious. The pickup when I used the keyword *friends*. She was afraid of leading me on. I was just an old friend that she now had the pleasure of pitying because of my adoption sob story. Had she not been dying in her last life, she never would have given me a chance. Beck was out of my league.

I ran my hands across my face and scrubbed my eyes. Would Sin City be my personal nightmare? Would I be "friend-zoned"? Had I really said *cool*?

CHAPTER 7

On the heels of my embarrassment, I had preparations to make before my trip with Beck and her friends. I needed to secure my position at the college as an attending student. I needed a home in Clover. And lastly, but possibly most important, I needed to go shopping. Sure, I should pick up a couple of shirts and swim trunks, but what I really needed was a birthday gift for Beck. An engagement ring would not suffice for a girl who couldn't remember.

I drank down the bitter, black hotel coffee as I swiped through job openings at the college. My laptop sprawled across my lap, and a pad of paper to my side that read "Student? Job?" The list was slim. I figured if I couldn't get in as a student, as the enrollment period had already closed, I could at least shoot for a job at Norton. Anything that gave me a purpose to be on campus, because the stalker look wasn't what I was going for.

The college was in search of a janitor and a math professor. Although I didn't enjoy math, I was good at it. Good enough to be a college professor. And I suppose if push came to shove, I could try for that position. Still, the chances were bleak without teaching credentials, and I didn't have time to ask Clouse to fabricate the necessary materials. I wasn't sure if he'd made it out of the bar that day anyway. If for some reason the university hired me for a position, I could twist my way out of telling Beck I was a student. Picking up the pad of paper to my side, I jotted down the details of the open position.

I flipped the page and wrote "home?" and revisited the houses I was looking at previously. Of course, they were both still for sale. Nothing moved quick in Clover, but if I wanted my story to be plausible, I had to. I made a couple of phone calls and scheduled the viewings later that evening with the real estate agent, Tina McFay. She sounded as if it would be her first viewing in a week or longer but didn't want to appear too open. She pushed me off until the evening. It worked out well, as I had errands to run anyway.

I got dressed in a new variation of the same clothing I had shoved in my backpack and set off. I felt the need to get to the college as soon as possible, but the simple fact that I didn't have clothing for an interview prompted me to go shopping first. The closest strip mall was nearly forty-five minutes away, and I spent the entire drive mulling over the perfect gift for Beck. I couldn't give her what I wanted most, and the more I thought about it, the more I realized my options were limited. Unless I wanted to be an ex-neighbor with a restraining order, I needed to settle on something simple. Flowers were always a pleasant choice, but they'd die, and it's not like she wanted to tote flowers around with her on the plane. A bracelet was too romantic for a supposed friend. Chocolate was an excellent choice, if it wouldn't melt. I must have run through two dozen terribly unfitting gift ideas by the time I arrived at the mall.

As I began weaving in and out of the shops, I noticed the demographics were eighty percent women. The men were either in tow with a girlfriend or hidden in groups of friends, and I wondered what all these people were doing off on a Friday afternoon. They couldn't possibly be shopping for fun, could they? A way to pass the time and empty their pockets in doing so? I browsed the store names above every door and passed on most. But when I walked by a store filled with things that sparkled, I stopped dead in my tracks. If I knew one thing, it was that girls liked things that sparkled. Like a moth drawn to light, girls had been pining after shiny objects since as far back as I could remember. And that was saying a lot.

I pulled the door open and entered the tiny shop filled with crystal objects. The air was still and stale. With little traffic to compete with, I immediately stole the attention of the store clerk, an elderly lady who was past the age of retirement but wouldn't have it any other way. Despite how high she had climbed on the ladder of life, she had more time than most. Her cheeks fought gravity and lifted into small painted red cheeks on her weathered face.

"Can I help you?" The woman asked, clasping her bony hands together. Right away, I could tell that this interaction may be the highlight of her week, and it was my duty as a Tethered Soul to make it count.

"I'd love some help. I need to get a special gift, but I'm not sure what I'm looking for." I walked up to a glass enclosure with tiered shelving and spinning trivets of glistening treasures.

"Well, you came to the right place! My name is Patsy, and I'll be helping you out today. Let's start with some questions. Who is the gift for? And what is the occasion?" Patsy asked. I could tell I'd be spending more time here than I would like, but the sooner I accepted it, the easier it would be. So, I shook off my impatience and gave Patsy the best customer interaction she'd have in a long while.

"Well, Patsy, it's an interesting story. Do you have time for a story?" My eyes glanced around the empty store, and I feared it appeared as mockery. Of course, she had the time. But Patsy's age-worn eyes didn't pick up on the subtlety.

"Oh, do tell me! I just love a good story."

"OK then. It begins with a girl . . ."

Patsy's eyes lit up. She was hungry for a real-life love story.

"We used to be neighbors when we were kids. I loved her then, when I was eight." I pulled out the picture of Beck and me on our second wedding from my wallet. This photo had a special place in my wallet, hidden behind a tri-folded blank check. The picture was worn and had a mark through the middle where it had been folded so many times before. The photograph was of our pretend backyard wedding.

Beck held her rabbit, and I wore a suit that extended well beyond my limbs.

Patsy gasped, bringing one hand to her stolen heart, and one shaky hand to the old photograph. It was among the few belongings I kept from my current childhood.

"Does she love you, too?"

"Well, see, that's the problem. My family moved that summer. We lost touch for so many years. I only recently ran into her by chance at a college we both attend."

"Oh!" Patsy made a high-pitched sound somewhere between a statement and a question. Her eyes glistened with the tears of hope.

"Yeah. I think it's fate . . . I really do," I said. And I wasn't lying. Beck and I were fated mates. Even if she didn't know it yet in this lifetime. We both knew in our last one. And I'd like to think we knew it as kids, too—when our subconscious ran wild and we weren't yet caged by plausibility.

"So, you want to give her a gift? I know just the one!" Patsy hobbled to a desk nearby and unlocked the glass lid. She lifted out a large crystal heart that came to a sharp point, and I couldn't help but to see the resemblance to my own beating heart with its sharp, possibly dangerous edge.

I smiled at the mere thought of handing Beck a large weighted heart for her birthday. I steepled my fingertips under my chin and pretended to consider Patsy's perfect pick.

"See, the thing is . . . I don't want to come off too strong," I said.

Patsy's eyes lowered to the heart in her hands. "I see . . ."

"It's her birthday, and actually, I think she has a boyfriend. So timing is important, and I don't know that this is the time to tell her I love her. Not just yet."

"Oh! Yes, that's good thinking." She brought her hand to her cheek and let her old eyes wander the shop in thought. I took a deep breath and let it out slowly. I wanted to look around the shop myself, but I knew letting her help me was more important. It was when Patsy had a second perfect pick that I realized I would have to buy something just to make her happy, and I would have to shop for Beck's birthday gift elsewhere, and I was OK with that.

"It's the perfect birthday gift for a girl in love," Patsy said.

"You know, I think you're right! It's perfect!" I stared down at the crystal bear holding a bouquet of pink balloons. I couldn't possibly give it to Beck.

"Isn't he the cutest bear? I'll wrap him up for you. She's going to love it." Patsy hobbled behind the register and wrapped the bear in white tissue paper. I lowered my forearms to the glass table between us and stretched my back. I let my eyes wander over the land of glimmer below until wandering was the last thing they wanted to do. My sights glued to a small crystal dragonfly no larger than a quarter. It had a green, beaded body and peridot wings. *That* was the perfect gift.

"Patsy? Can you throw in that little dragonfly too?" I pointed to the corner of the display where the dragonfly rest.

"Of course, dear!"

I wondered if it would mean anything to Beck. If she would look at it and know it was something more special than eye candy.

Patsy wrapped up my gifts with the speed of a tortoise and then checked me out in the same fashion. I glanced at my watch. I'd spent an hour in the store. I had to pick up the pace if I wanted to get to the college and make it in time for the house tours that evening.

"Thank you, Patsy. I couldn't have found the perfect gift for my girl without you." I said.

"Oh, dear. You go get her, you hear?" Patsy said.

I winked at her before exiting and sliding my sunglasses back over my eyes.

I dashed into the first shop that displayed men's clothing in the window and picked up three collared shirts, two T-shirts, and an extra pair of jeans. A black blazer also found its way into my hands to help with my first impression, if I was fortunate enough to snag an interview. My sizes never changed, and it made shopping effortless. I left the store carrying a large paper bag and one tiny, pink, plastic one. I knew I should take the time to get a proper pair of dress shoes, but I was feeling the pressure to move on with my day.

I had picked up my pace, but soon found myself in the wrong place at the wrong time. Right as I was about to step off the curb into the parking lot, a nearby pretzel stand caused my stomach to rumble and my mouth to water. I checked my watch again. I barely had time to grab a quick pretzel and soda before my drive to the college. As soon as I made the decision to wait in the line, my sense of urgency dissipated. It had happened to me many times over my past lives. Tugging, pulling, urges to be somewhere or do something. They never made sense . . . until they did. Till I discovered the true meaning. More often than not, I wondered if I was merely a pawn in someone else's scheme.

It was my turn to order, and I took a step forward to meet the young teen working the register. A tall striped hat was part of her uniform—the worst part.

"I'll have a pretzel and soda to go, please," I said.

"Name?"

"Easton."

"That will be seven-fifty."

I gave her a ten, and when I received the change back, I dumped it in her tip jar. She thanked me with a smile. I waited for my order to be complete, and in doing so I unwrapped the crystal bear. I hadn't planned to give it to Beck, and I certainly didn't want to tote it around with me in my backpack. I examined the bear in my hand and concluded that Patsy was right; it was the perfect gift. Just not for Beck. I looked around at all the people passing by the pretzel stand and placed the bear on top of an open table in plain sight. The tightness in my stomach finally put me to ease as I left the gift where it needed to be. I turned my back on it and waited for my order, realizing I wasn't hungry at all.

It wasn't long before I heard the gasp of a girl behind me. No doubt, it was at the sight of the bear on top of the deserted table. A gentle tug at the corner of my lips pulled upward, and pride replaced the tension I had felt in my chest. It was in these unique moments, few and far between, that I stopped wondering why I was a Tethered Soul, and simply was.

"Oh my god! Hanna, look!"

"Whose is that?"

"I don't know. It was just sitting here?"

"OK, that's . . . weird!"

"Do you think . . ."

"We should turn it in. It's clearly somebody's . . ."

"I think it's . . . yours?"

There was a moment of silence before I could hear the muffled bout of emotion threatening to boil over. I wondered what the bear meant to her. Had her mother given her a teddy bear with pink balloons? Had she bought a crystal bear for her best friend or a sister before they passed? Could it be the same make and model? I didn't need to know what it meant to the girl to know that it was special to her. The stifled cry was contagious, causing my throat to burn. I knew exactly how she felt as I held back the pain I shared with a person I'd never met but knew had loved and lost.

"Easton! Order for Easton!"

My attention snapped back to the food, and I gathered my bags and my pretzel to go. When I turned to leave, the girls passed me on the way to the counter and asked, "Do you know if this belongs to anyone? It was sitting at that table over there." They both pointed to the table in unison. Only one girl had blood-shot eyes, and equal parts pain and hope streaming down her cheeks.

The teen working the checkout replied, "No. Nobody has sat at that table all day. If you want it, it's yours."

I'd passed just before hearing them gasp once more, and I walked away with a smile on my face that was deep enough to touch my heart.

CHAPTER 8

Now that I had Beck's birthday gift squared away, it was time to secure myself a reason for showing up at the college. Then, if I was lucky enough, a home as well. But when I found myself sitting in front of the dean, my hope all but slipped away.

"I'm so sorry. You will have to wait for open enrollment. We're not currently accepting students. And the math professor's position was filled this morning, Mr. Green." The dean, a woman late into her fifties with ebony skin and a brilliant blue scarf tied around her neck, examined my resume. It was the best prefabrication I could make with such brief notice.

"I understand. Perhaps the professor will need a teacher's aide? I could be of help," I countered, pulling at my blazer collar, hoping I looked sharp.

"We have all the aides we need at the moment. But check back with us. You never know what the future holds." She clasped her hands together and rested them on her desk. A sure sign that she was ready for me to leave her office. I clenched my jaw. Not yet ready to give up.

"Are there any job openings at the college? Anything?" I asked, sounding more desperate than I intended.

"Well, there is one . . ." I raised my eyebrows and leaned forward in my chair. "We *are* in need of a janitor."

". . . Anything . . . *else*?"

"No, Mr. Green. That's all."

I sighed. I needed a reason to be here. I needed time. Time to grow with her. Time to uncover the truth with her. Time to make her love me again. And I couldn't do that if I didn't attend the college.

I cleared my throat, trying one last option. "I spoke with the counselor earlier who said you may have room for another student and that you might consider an exception?" It was a blatant lie, of course. The counselor told me just the opposite, in fact.

The dean furrowed her eyebrows and I could tell her trust towards me was fading.

"For a donation of course." It was a Hail Mary. I had to try. I watched her expression change from one of annoyance to slight interest. I had to strike while the iron was hot. "Perhaps—"

"Mr. Green, with all due respect, I don't think you're capable of a bribe bountiful enough to bend the rules. Now, if you don't mind, I have quite a bit of work to do, and I'd prefer to get back to it. Thank you for coming in." With that, she picked up her pen and began to work while I was still seated in her office.

My mind raced in circles. Should I take the janitorial

position? Would that get me closer to Beck? Should I donate the money I took from Clouse and forgo buying a home in Clover? Somehow all of my options were terrible. None managed to inch out above the others. I ran my hands through my hair and stood to make my exit. I walked slowly, giving myself the time to change my mind within the seconds I had left in the dean's office. When I heard her voice again, I knew it was fate giving me a fighting chance.

"Mr. Green?" The dean asked.

A smile spread across my face and I spun on my heels to face her. "Yes, Dean?"

"The tag is sticking out of your blazer collar." The dean smiled as she watched my face heat. By the time the door had closed behind me, my mouth was parched, I had no security at Norton, and I was utterly humiliated. I reached behind my collar and ripped the tag off throwing it in the trash on my way past the counselor.

By the time I reached the parking lot, I'd come up with a Plan B. I wasn't proud of Plan B, but when push came to shove, I had no other choice. I'd show up on the days Beck went to class, and I'd pretend I had class too. I'd lie. *Simply lie*, until one day—and hopefully, that day was sooner than later—she would remember me. Our life. Our love. And I could be in her life beyond school. But until then, it looked like I had some acting to do. Luckily for me, I had practice.

I must have played the exact moment the dean smiled at my embarrassment a hundred times before I arrived at the Clover Real Estate's office of Tina McFay. Since I hadn't just donated my savings to weasel my way into college, I would have enough for a down payment on a home. I wrapped my hand around the cold metal doorknob, and just as I pulled the door open, Tina just about fell out. She stumbled on her heels before standing tall and adjusting her clothing.

"You must be Easton! So nice to meet you. Thank you for coming in today!"

I shook her hand, which was petite and warm. She was attractive enough to be on a magazine cover. And if I had to choose which type of magazine, I'd have to say swim. Her pencil skirt hugged her curves, which resembled an hourglass figure. Her teeth were perfectly straight and perfectly white, and her hair was long and lustrous.

"We have two houses to look at this afternoon. Let me just grab my notes and we can get a move on it." Tina turned to grab her notes, and my eyes dropped slightly. I wondered how much her looks played into her job. Did she sell more houses because she was easy on the eyes?

I took a deep breath and examined my surroundings. Her office could have been a spread in a magazine, but not from a swim edition—more like home decor. I gave my head a shake, dispelling my thoughts as I moved to the entryway table, on which sat a stunning bouquet of tulips and a bowl of etched wooden balls. Everything matched and flowed effortlessly. It was probably a language Beck understood, being in graphic design, but all I could do was appreciate it.

"Do you stage the houses you sell?" I asked.

"I do! Most of them need it!" Tina said as she shoved a notebook into her bag.

"I like what you've done here." I vaguely pointed to the

shelves that were lined with photographs in heavy farmhouse framing.

"Thank you! It's a fun pastime. Are you ready?"

"Yeah!" I clapped my hands and then followed Tina to her car. When I stepped inside her car, I was thankful that it was clean and odor-free. It was a simple task, but one that was unattainable by most.

"So the first house we're going to is the smaller one. It's about twelve hundred square feet, but it has a nice location. It's at the end of a cul-de-sac, which personally, I enjoy. And if you plan on having children, I just think it's a safer option, as well."

I thought about it. Children. I'd never once seriously considered it. The first time I died, I was just a child myself. After I found out what I was, or more rather, *who* I was, I didn't think it would be fair to have children. Now, after all of these years, I was positive I was incapable of having kids. The chances of a mishap would have happened by now, and no such thing had. I was sterile alright.

"I'd love a family one day," I said.

Tina smiled a warm and endearing smile. "I would too."

My stomach dropped with unease. "I already have the engagement ring, so as soon as the time is right, I'm going to ask my girlfriend to marry me. I doubt she will want to wait long to have kids." I made my stance clear as day. Tina's eyes lost their sparkle. But the uneasiness in my stomach went away.

We pulled up to the first house. Option A. It was indeed tiny—old too. Red brick peeked out from behind the overgrown weeds and covered the bottom portion of the house. An abandoned scooter rest against a tree. The driveway was long and skinny, and the windows needed replacement.

"I know it's not much on the outside, but if you can imagine a facelift, and some yard work, I think this would be a beautiful fixer-upper." Tina framed the house with her hands. I nodded, unsure if I could see her vision.

We stepped inside, and the stale smell of mildew escaped into the open air. I looked at Tina with a doubtful expression, but she charged forward with confidence.

"This is the living room!" she said. I stared at the brown shag carpet, and my eyes flicked to various stains, which reminded me of the spots on a cow's hide.

It couldn't have been more than ten steps into the home before Tina said, "And this is the kitchen," in the same cheerful tone. Small was an understatement; we didn't need to walk any further than the front door to see the kitchen, living room, and dining room. In fact, I could see the backyard from where I stood as well. Though larger than an apartment, this house felt smaller than a cardboard box. I followed Tina into each room, the tour lasting a full two minutes. When she finally stopped to examine my face, she agreed we should look at Option B.

Once outside in the fresh evening air, I took a deep breath. Expanding my lungs as full as they could stretch. The smell of overgrown grass never smelled so clean. A part of me wanted to stop Tina right then and there and tell her that whatever the second house looked like, I'd take it, because it couldn't be worse than this one. But in true Easton fashion . . . I was wrong.

Option B was *worse*. The house was larger, which was nice, and the smell was at least tolerable. But it was . . . sinister. And if I had to guess, I'd say the house was haunted. As if the subtle constriction of my throat and the icy pockets of stale air weren't enough to convince me, Tina had to disclose the multiple deaths that had taken place over the last few years in the house, and it was more than any one home should endure. I wondered what mysteries lay inside. No, I had enough on my mind; I didn't need to lie awake at night and feel encapsulated by the darkness and evil that lived there. I'd rather spend my free time ripping out brown carpet and breathing in mold.

To say I was disappointed with how my day turned out was an understatement. Although I found the perfect gift for Beck's birthday, I had no job, no tie to her schedule at the college, and now, the only two homes in Clover were nothing short of atrocious. But if I didn't attend Norton as I said and I didn't have a home where I said, then what *did* I have? I was desperate to make my story plausible. Desperate to give myself a shot.

Just when I thought I had no chance in hell of ever laying down roots in Clover, I had to remind myself of the ending to my recurring nightmare. The boulder had crushed my leg, or so I thought. Despite the momentum it had from barreling down the hill, however, something had stopped it dead in its tracks—just above my ankle. When the fear subsided, I could see that there was a perfect tunnel etched into the perfectly round boulder. My foot was free, and I could slide out unscathed. I crawled out from underneath the boulder and I stood inches from it, marveling at the hazard that had never touched me but almost killed me.

I had to remind myself that losing the ring wasn't the end, Beck forgetting me wasn't the end, and this wouldn't be how my story ended either. It was then that I pictured Beck wearing a hard hat and a tool belt. It's when I saw her laughing in the kitchen with a spatula. And it was when I saw her running through the tiny house wearing nothing but a bedsheet that I put an offer in on the house.

I came in low, even lower than what the house was worth, but Tina said that the home had been on the market for a year, and had no offers to date. We were sure my offer would be accepted. And at the end of the day, Tina would have some cash in her pocket, and I would have one less lie to carry on my shoulders.

CHAPTER 9

$\mathcal{I}$ counted down the days until the trip in both anticipation and dread alike. I couldn't wait to spend more time with Beck. There was a burning in my belly that told me I would inch my way closer to her heart if I had the time to do so. I couldn't think of a better way than to celebrate our birthdays together on a weekend away. But a nagging sensation gnawed at my thoughts, never letting me forget that Nolan wouldn't be far away. Behind every smile, every shared moment, and every glitter of hope, Nolan's eyes would burrow into me like those of a blood-sucking tick.

The funny part was, I couldn't blame the guy. He had impeccable taste. It only bothered me that he didn't feel the way I did for Beck. How could he? Our bond was something no college fling could come close to matching. Still, somewhere deep inside me, and unrelated to my conscious thoughts, I feared our untouchable bond wouldn't be enough. Or possibly never discovered. And it was foolish if I thought a crystal dragonfly would be the gift that kept on giving. No, it had to be something more. A kiss, perhaps?

I stumbled over my own two feet at the very thought of kissing Beck again, and I looked around to see if anyone had caught my blunder. If they had, they didn't care to make a mockery of me. It was about time for Beck's lunch, and I sat waiting on the bench she frequented. When her friend Brooklyn spotted me, she came to keep me company.

"Hey there. How are you today?" Brooklyn asked. Her long dark hair was parted down the middle and brushed slightly in front of her eye.

"Just another day in paradise," I said.

Brooklyn laughed, shaking off my sarcasm as she sat down. "I heard you're going to Sin City with us next weekend. Are you excited?"

"Yeah, I can't wait. It'll be nice to get out of this town and see the city." I had lied so many times. Pretended I was naive or inexperienced. It flowed out of me like the air expelled from my lungs, and half of the time, I never even realized it. It was a means of survival and nothing more . . . but it could prove the barrier that kept me from getting close to others.

"Me too! I've never been there. So excited!" Brooklyn said in a high-pitched tone. I looked up to catch her eyes, which were so warm and golden, they reminded me of spun honey, but that wasn't even the most interesting part. It was the boredom reflected in her eyes as she claimed to be excited that interested me the most.

"Hey," Nolan said as he took a seat.

"Hey," Brooklyn responded.

"So, what do you guys do in Sin City? Do you gamble?" I asked.

"I just drink, man. Maybe drink by the pool during the day?" Nolan said. I was slowly peeling back the multiple layers of Nolan, and the more I did, the more that hope crowded out my insecurities.

"I'm not twenty-one yet," said Brooklyn, "but I've got a fake ID, so I'm covered."

Beck kissed Nolan on the cheek, and he swatted her on the rear, making her yelp and drawing attention from those around us. I tried not to show a reaction of any kind. "Can I see it?" I asked Brooklyn.

"See what?" Beck asked, sitting down and pulling her bag onto her lap.

"My ID." Brooklyn handed me her ID from across the table. I looked at it closely for telltale signs of being a fake but couldn't find any. It was as real as any other I'd seen.

"Wow, that's legit. Where did you get it?" I asked.

"Oh, I have a guy." Brooklyn placed her hand under her chin and posed like a cherub. I laughed and wondered how far from the truth it really was.

"And your friend, James, does he have one too?"

"No, Brooklyn is the baby of the bunch. James is . . . what? Twenty-two? Twenty-three? I think he started at Norton late," Beck said.

"He didn't start late. He's just too dumb to pass his classes!" Nolan barked.

"Stop that!" Beck smacked him with the back of her hand. "James is actually very smart."

Nolan laughed out loud, "Are you serious? Have you met James? He can't sit still long enough to study! He's probably never read a book!"

I looked to Brooklyn during the quarrel, and she offered me an eye-roll. "Where is James? Does he go to school here?"

"Yes, but our classes don't align." I nodded, eager to make up my own theories about the man they called James.

A girl walked by on her cell phone, giving everyone a quick wave before meeting up with a guy. "Oh, that's Payton. She's coming to Sin City too," Beck pointed to the girl. Nolan seemed to take a particular interest, but I preferred to watch Beck lick the lid of her yogurt. I pretended to listen to Brooklyn talk about something that happened in her class today, but the truth was, I was too busy stealing glances at Beck. Only when Nolan stood up abruptly and crumpled up his lunch bag to throw in the trash can did I turn my head to peek at Payton. Her arms were wrapped around the guy's neck, and his hands rested dangerously low on her back. I watched Nolan slam his lunch into the trash. Beck's eyes flickered about. I didn't know how unstable her relationship was, but I gathered it may be rocky by the time this group was several drinks deep—in a place called Sin City, nonetheless.

I showed up on Thursday at Norton University, just long enough to catch Beck passing through the halls. I told her I had an errand to run at lunch, but that I'd see her at the airport. I didn't have errands to run, but I did fear wearing out my welcome. Figuring if I was going to be with Beck for a full weekend, I'd better give her a little space now. And if all went as planned, the statement "Absence makes the heart grow fonder," would ring true.

I spent the day at the old dive bar where I used to meet Clyde the second time around. I was reminded of the evenings I labored to make up for leaving him behind in an unfit home. He never did let me in, and ultimately, I realized we were more alike than I ever imagined us to be. Still, I wished I had a third chance to make it right. Simon had been nowhere in sight. I only hoped that he had moved on to a better life. And if I didn't find him in this one, perhaps I would see him in the next handful of lives to come. Joey no longer worked at the bar, which was to be expected at his age, and all the regulars had been replaced. Somehow, it felt more like home to me than the place I'd grown up. I knew that when I sat down in that dark grungy bar—whether or not I recognized the faces around me— that Clyde was with me.

After showering the stench of smoke and booze off my body, I packed a bag for the trip. It was nearly everything I had with me when I moved out of my home. Precisely enough to get by and not an ounce more. I sent an e-mail to Tina about the house and dabbled in stocks before I set my alarm for the morning flight. And when I closed my eyes that night, I hoped I would return to Clover a different man.

I filed onto the plane, careful not to bump the shoulders and elbows of the already seated passengers. The seating was open, and it was clear by the order in which the plane was being boarded that I wouldn't be sitting with Beck. She took a middle seat, her friend Payton by the window, and Nolan on the aisle. I squeezed past Nolan as he placed his carry-on overhead and found the second-closest seats available. Behind them and across the aisle sat James, Brooklyn, and I. Brooklyn would have been my second choice, and I could tell that the feeling was mutual.

James was a shorter, husky guy. His eyes were as dark as the mole on his left cheek. For what he lacked in height, though, he made up for in noise. I knew the key to his affection was none other than attention. It was the simplest personality to crack. I'd known my fair share of attention-seekers. Loud and boisterous, sometimes reckless and unforgiving. The need to be seen and heard trumped every other need . . . or so it would seem. But somewhere deep down was the need that always came up short—the one that was unmet and hidden away. I expected James to be no different, but what made him the most unique was not how bright his candle burned but how short the wick was. He wouldn't live a long life.

The flight attendant gave her spiel about safety, and though I had it memorized, I stared vaguely in her direction so I wouldn't appear rude. You didn't have to be an attention-seeker to want to be heard or respected; that was a shared personality trait amongst them all. Myself included.

Brooklyn fiddled with the air spout above us, and James opened his backpack, revealing a plethora of snacks. Had I not known better, I'd say he robbed the gift shop.

Brooklyn looked at me with a sympathetic eye. "It's a shame, huh?" she said, hurt filling her eyes.

I looked between her and James, and my skin turned warm. "What is?"

Brooklyn's gold eyes shifted, and she returned to being the carefree girl that I saw most of the time. "That he didn't get us any chocolate. Oh, can I have one of these?" She pointed to a roll of Sprees.

"Yeah, yeah! Take whatever you want," James said.

Brooklyn picked her candy, and James took his time digging through the salty and sweet for the perfect choice. I ran my hands through my hair, closing my eyes. It was all too clear that I was stressed. It was a slip-up, and I hadn't meant to show it.

Of course, Brooklyn would catch the one time I let my act fall for a brief breath in silence. "It's OK. I get scared too. I brought some shots. Let's take one now, so takeoff won't be so bad—because that's the worst part. Well, that and landing," Brooklyn said.

Even though fear of flying was not my issue, a shot may still be the fix.

"That sounds great. Thanks." A little something to take the edge off was exactly what I needed.

Brooklyn pulled out six shots. When the flight attendant turned her back, I passed three over to Nolan.

"Bottoms up!" James said and downed his shot. Brooklyn smiled an encouraging smile and wished me a happy birthday before she gulped half of the clear liquid, shaking her head a multitude of times before going at it again. I swallowed mine whole.

I wasn't much of a drinker. Not in this life, and not in most before. There was a time—a life—when I tried desperately to escape my cyclical, never-ending existence. But the drinking never fixed the loneliness, and to be honest, it just made me an asshole. That life went by in a blur. I was a burden on society, the worst part of many people's day. And then it ended. I died recklessly, just as I had lived. And then I started anew. When I looked back on that life, I always came up with the same question: what was the point? Since then, I'd rather feel the pain and be able to live with myself at the end of the day.

"Oh, God! It's *so* bad! How did you guys drink the whole thing like that?" Brooklyn stomped her feet against the floor like a child throwing a tantrum. Her twenty years of age were reflected in her acquired taste that was yet to be. It wasn't until a shiver ripped through her body that I laughed at her, lifting my mood. The warm liquid chased away the worry that I carried onto the plane with me, and I was so grateful that I asked for another.

James, Brooklyn, and I took another shot, this time not sharing with the other three. Brooklyn buried her face in the crook of her elbow and coughed as James and I laughed. No matter what happened on this trip, I was along for the ride; and for the first time since being invited, I was OK with that.

CHAPTER 10

The plane took off, throwing us back against our seats. Brooklyn grabbed hold of my wrist and then James's too. She scrunched her eyes closed tight, and I tried to comfort her the only way I knew how. I rattled off statistics.

"The chance of this plane crashing is only one in five-point-four million. You have a greater chance of being struck by lightning or mauled by a wombat. Just take a deep breath . . . and maybe another shot. Before you know it, we'll be in Vegas." While I may have included some of my own statistics, I was sure she wasn't listening to me either way.

Brooklyn took several deep breaths, and sometime after her third and fourth shot, she relaxed. Her body was heavy and her lips loose. She leaned in and divulged secrets about her friends. I soaked up every word like a sponge while James snored against the window.

"Payton's always had a thing for Nolan, even after they

broke up in high school. She just can't seem to let him go. She won't admit it, of course, because Becca is her friend, so she pretends to be happy for them, but really, she's jealous as shit!" The smell of vodka lingered on her breath as the truth spilled out.

"So, is Beck serious with Nolan?" I asked.

Brooklyn sighed and looked up to the ceiling of the cabin. "Um, I mean, it's complicated. They're not like *exclusive*, if you will, but"—she took a moment to pop a Spree in her mouth and mull it over in her head—"I honestly think Beck likes him more than he likes her."

As much as I was happy that their bond was breakable, I still ached for Beck that she'd not been loved properly.

"I mean, look at him. He's gorgeous. Who wouldn't fall all over his feet?"

I looked in their direction, and a pang of jealousy drifted over me. "Do you like him, too?" I asked.

"Me?" Brooklyn pointed at the remainder of the Sprees, an extension of her finger, to her chest. "I wouldn't. He's not my type. He's . . . well, maybe? I mean, no! No, I don't like him. I like to look at him, but that's not the same thing. Huh, I'm saying too much aren't I?"

"No, you are saying just the right amount, actually."

We laughed, and I could tell she wasn't worried about me keeping her secrets.

"Can I tell you something?" I said. After much deliberation, I concluded Brooklyn put a lot of weight on trust. And though she was spilling everyone's secrets at the moment, I could tell it was more to do with the occupation of keeping her mind off the plane crashing than the alcohol erasing her inhibitions. Plus, the gossip was child's play compared to the secrets she really held dear. Her soul was buried at the depths of the ocean, and I wondered what had put it there. A trauma was my guess, but I wouldn't pry, as it was none of my business. The way to her heart was trust, and I knew how to be loyal. Brooklyn sensed as much, and I assumed some of that was why she'd chosen to open up to me.

"Anything!" Her eyebrows lifted in curiosity.

"Don't tell anyone, but"—her eyes focused on mine, the gold glimmer warm and inviting—"I always felt deep down in my gut that Beck was my soulmate. And one day, I plan to marry her," I said, all acting aside. As if two marriages weren't enough, I wanted a third. A traditional one.

Brooklyn sighed at the depth of my seriousness. "Oh my god! I got chills! I totally believe in that kind of stuff!" She lifted her arm between us, and it was covered in tiny goosebumps. "You know, I see it. It all makes sense. So much sense." She scratched her head, smiling off into the distance. "Now, can I tell you a secret?"

I leaned in, all ears. "What?"

"She's the missing piece to your puzzle." My brows pulled together, not understanding. Brooklyn pointed at Beck. "It's her. She's your missing piece," Brooklyn said in a whisper with a slight lisp, then gazed off in Beck's direction.

I followed her line of sight, and watching as Nolan lowered his head to Beck's. I was grateful that I could only see the back of her chair. Her soft giggle lifted into the air, and my stomach dipped, knowing that I'd not been the one to make her laugh. Still, through the pain, I enjoyed the sound.

Just as I was about to ask Brooklyn to elaborate, she turned to me, announcing she needed to use the restroom. I pressed my knees together and shifted to the side as Brooklyn straddled me ungracefully and crawled out of the row, making her way to the back of the plane.

I closed the hotel door behind me, thankful that Beck's room was adjacent to mine but more than a little disturbed that she was sharing it with Nolan. Brooklyn and Payton were placed in a room down the hall, and James was on the first floor, which suited his need to be amongst the bustling casino guests and flashing lights.

I unpacked, trying not to think about all the things Nolan was doing to Beck at the very moment, and I couldn't be more grateful that we didn't end up with adjoining rooms. Sharing a wall would be my new nightmare, making the boulder pale in comparison.

I tried to dispel the thoughts and unwelcome images with a shower. This couldn't really be my second life with Beck? I had amounted to nothing more than supporting best friend. Her birthday twin. Her old neighbor. Did she really not remember me? Our entire life before this?

I willed myself to remember my second life. It was a long time ago, and while I remembered that it was more difficult to understand the situation I had come upon then, I didn't have the clarity I needed to assess Beck's situation. I didn't know how to uncover the hidden memories because I had forgotten what it was like.

I dressed and spent a few extra moments messing with my hair. When it protested, I gave up. It didn't matter anyway. My eyes searched the mirror, looking for answers regarding how I ended up here and how I could find my way out. But the reflection only mocked me with unruly hair and dark shadows under my eyes. I was startled by the loud knock on my hotel door, and I left the man in the mirror for another time.

"Ooh! Don't you look handsome!" Brooklyn said as she stumbled into my room on the arm of Payton.

Payton was a cute girl with an athletic body; short and muscular. Her hair was long and mousy brown. It was thin and dry, and despite her toned body, I could tell that she didn't take care of herself.

"Where is Ev . . . Beck?" I asked the girls.

"She's probably in pound town right about now," Payton said, rolling her eyes.

Brooklyn backhanded her shoulder a little harder than I think she meant to, and I could see that my secret was already out by the way Payton responded with wide regretful eyes.

I turned away from the girls as they made themselves comfortable on my bed, and I stared out the window to the streets below. The people were like ants swarming the city. The girls talked about their plans for the night, and I only half-listened while the other half of me was with the people out my window. It was easier to think about them than "pound town." I ran my hand through my hair, disheveling it further.

Much more time passed than I would have liked before Beck and Nolan appeared. His hair was ruffled and his shirt wrinkled. The sight of him made my throat restrict, and I wondered how I would possibly make it through an entire weekend away with these lust birds. My prior resolve to settle in for the ride faded away with the buzz I had long ago, leaving me with a much more sober and somber tone.

"Let's get some drinks at the bar and do a little gambling while we wait for James. I've been dying to play the slots," Beck said as she swiped through her phone. My eyes trailed from her silver earrings swinging by her neck down to the curves of her thigh before darting away the moment her gaze lifted.

"Why don't we go to the buffet? Ribs, shrimp, pizza, all on one plate!" Nolan said holding his arms out as if there were no possible way anyone could refuse the thought of a heaping plate of mismatched food. I couldn't help it when the image of him hunching over a plate of meat scraps crossed my mind. How could she possibly be attracted to him? And now Payton and Brooklyn too? I watched him, my jaw slightly dropping as I scrambled to find the answers to his appeal, and finally resolved to the idea that his lure was not meant for me to see.

"OK, well, you do you . . . I'm going to get a margarita at the bar. We can meet up later." Payton threw her hands up in the air and walked out of the room. Brooklyn laughed and stumbled behind her, leaving Beck, Nolan, and I in an uncomfortable circle of awkward silence. Not soon enough,

Nolan answered a phone call, taking several steps away. It wasn't much, but I felt the privacy between Beck and I return.

"How do you want to spend your twenty-first birthday?" I asked.

Beck slid her phone into her bag and took a seat on the edge of my bed. "I don't know. I just want to order a drink at a bar. At a pool. At a club. I'm going to be so mad if they don't card me! That's all I really want, to be carded. I want to flash my ID as much as possible this weekend." She leaned back onto her elbows, exposing an inch of flesh and the crevice of her belly button. My heart lurched, and I forced my gaze up to the ceiling.

"I'll make sure that they card you. Everyone in this forsaken city will think you're a minor, if that's what you want for your birthday," I said, avoiding the length of her body on top of my bed. Beck laughed, eyeing me suspiciously.

"What about you, birthday boy? How do you want to spend your twenty-first birthday?"

I wanted to spend it with her. Just as she was now. A smile on her face and a sparkle in her eyes. I wanted her to remember me. I wanted Nolan to be no more than history, and I wanted my future promised with a ring on her finger. "I . . . I want to try my hand at poker," I said as I felt the weight of my shallow lie. Though, it would be nice to pocket some cash for the weekend.

"Do you know how to play?"

"I used to play with my . . . grandpa." And for a moment I was back in the bar playing poker with Clyde and his drunken buddies. His foul mouth would always run, and his tough exterior never wavered, but the times that he laughed so hard he slapped the poker table and the chips would rumble were enough to keep me coming back time and time again. My lips twitched with a smile.

"Maybe you could teach me?" Beck's eyebrows raised, and the smile spread well beyond my face.

Nolan ended his call and informed Beck they were going to the buffet. Beck invited me, but I didn't need to look at Nolan to feel the radiating disapproval from him. I settled, promising to teach Beck how to gamble after their dinner.

We split after the elevator, and I made my way to the casino floor. The room was buzzing with cigarette smoke and high stakes. Most were drowning in the disappointment of lost wages, leaving few with chips in their pockets or optimism in their hearts. I spotted Brooklyn and Payton at the bar talking to a couple of men; I'd leave them to it.

After evaluating several tables, I found one to my liking and pulled up a seat. Three players, all men, and a dealer who was probably in her late sixties, early seventies. She wore a short skirt and a revealing top as part of her uniform. Her lips puckered with the wrinkles that only a long-time smoker earned in due time.

"Yes, pull up a seat, hon," she said in a splintered voice.

I joined the table, and the dealer counted me in. Two of the men eyed me, and the third didn't notice me at all. I was pretty good at poker because of my ability to read people, but I cursed myself for never taking the time to learn how to count cards. As the game began, I committed to learning in this lifetime, starting with this very game.

Time was lost as if in an alternate universe. It was a phenomenon that happened only to gamblers, and as I sat at that table, I was not immune to its powers. That's why I was surprised when Beck placed her hand on my shoulder some three hours later.

"There you are! I've been looking all over for you!"

"You have?" I looked around. I was nearly four thousand dollars up, and there was a new player at the table.

"Yeah, we finished dinner a while ago and we've all been at the bar."

I looked back as far as my eyes could stretch. There in the bar was a small group of people gathered around James as he told a lavish story with so much animation, he had an open ring around him further than his arms could reach. I returned my attention to the table and reaped my winnings, thanking the dealer with a tip.

"Wow, you're really good!"

"Oh, just beginner's luck," I said. Beck's brows knitted as I pocketed my chips. We started back to her friends, but before we got far, she asked if I knew how to play the slots.

"I don't play, but I'm sure we could figure it out together. Sit down, let's see," I said.

Beck took a seat at a nearby mermaid slot machine. It was her third serious consideration, and I poked fun of her every time she switched machines. She cracked every knuckle on both of her hands before shaking them out. The stress radiated off of her in sheets.

"Are you OK?"

"Yeah! I'm just getting ready," Beck said.

I laughed at her theatrics. "Alright then. If you're ready to lose some money, put the coin in, and pull the lever."

Beck looked at me like I was deceiving her. "Is that it?" she asked.

I shrugged, "Um, maybe push one of these buttons?"

"Oh my god! You don't even know how to use this thing!" Beck swatted at me, and I jumped backward when all I really wanted was to dive in close. Our playful banter was like a small sense of recognition. Her welcoming an old friend back into her life. The closer I got to her, the more I craved it. We messed around on the slots for a little while until Beck was sick of losing her money. Then, we took some of my winnings, and I taught her how to play roulette.

"Make sure you card this one. I don't think she's old enough to be here!" I said to the man in charge of the roulette.

He looked at me, unamused. "I'll need to see *both* of your IDs." Beck sucked in a quick breath and snickered into my shoulder. We handed our IDs to the man, who was twice my size. He gave them back with slight annoyance.

"Sir, I think your hair is on fleak!" Beck said. My eyes widened as I looked back to the man's head of thinning hair. Though I couldn't see the top, I was still sure that there would be a round balding patch. He frowned, causing Beck's cheeks to turn crimson.

"I thought it was a compliment. It was supposed to make him feel good. It doesn't work for me. It never has,"

Beck whispered, turning her face away from the man. Beck didn't know that she was still loud enough for him to hear, but he and I did.

I smiled an apologetic smile and handed him our bet. At least some things were still there hidden within Beck, and I briefly wondered if the alcohol would be the key that unlocked even more yet. After much deliberation, Beck chose black, and I think she enjoyed it more than pulling the lever on the slots. It was something in the way her eyes sparkled that made me want to reach out behind the nape of her neck and kiss her long and deep. But when I realized I couldn't, my smile began to fade as my eyes lingered on her lips.

Beck looked up at me after we lost, catching the desire in my eyes. She bit her lip, meeting my gaze before breaking. "Come on, let's get back to the others. I don't think you can afford to teach me any more games," Beck said as she grabbed my arm and led me away.

I followed her back to her friends, leaning into her arm, and when she stumbled, I was there to catch her. If I hadn't expected to see Nolan around the corner, I would have kept my hand wrapped around her tight; but that wasn't the case. The small group in the bar had downsized, and only James and a petite but equally outgoing girl remained. Several empty shot glasses fell over and rolled around on the table when James brought his fist down in a fit of laughter. My brows shot up as I counted.

"Where's everyone at?" Beck asked James.

James appeared surprised to see us, and it was clear that we were interrupting his conversation. "Oh, I don't know.

They left a while ago." James vaguely waved to the exit sign. His eyes were red and glossy.

Beck took out her phone and stepped away to make a call. She must be reaching out to Nolan. I turned back to the table before me, and James and his new friend were carrying on as if I was no longer present.

I thrust my hands into my pockets and looked around the bar. One gentleman in particular caught my eye. He was a little older than the rest of the crowd. Forties perhaps. He sat alone, red hair resting to the side of his face. I didn't have to see his eyes to know he was a Tethered Soul. I could feel it. The same way someone knows when they're being watched, even though, presumably, nobody's in the room with them. I simply knew that in this bar full of strangers, he and I were the same. He'd lived many lives before, and his energy was palpable. The tortured pain of loneliness so thick I could reach out and touch it. On the contrary, Beck's was weak. So weak that she didn't even believe it to be true, and had I not known her in our last life, I wouldn't have believed it either.

"I can't get a hold of anyone. I think I'm going to turn in for the night." I could see the disappointment etched in Beck's face.

"What!? You can't do that! It's your birthday! You've got to celebrate!" I grabbed her hands and raised them into the air, forcing her to cheer for herself. It worked, but not for long. Her smile was fleeting.

"Well, I don't know what to do. I mean, I don't know where everyone is."

"What does everyone have to do with anything?" I said,

trying not to let her see my disappointment. I wasn't enough. Not yet.

"Well, what do *you* want to do? It's your birthday too!" she said.

"I would take it personally if you ditched me on my birthday. Let's go have some fun! If not for you, then do it for me!" I knew it would work. She couldn't let someone down.

"OK! Yeah, you're right. I'm in! What are we doing?" Beck pushed the pale hair out of her face and rubbed her hands together in anticipation. A second wind.

I used this opportunity to take a page out of my playbook. "You know, I've always wanted to go bungee jumping, and I think that can be done off one of the skyscrapers here." My stomach knotted while I said it. The last thing I wanted to do was jump off a building, but if I thought that Beck's life would be enriched by doing so—and I did—I would jump right alongside her.

"Really!? Oh my god! I've always wanted to do that!" Her eyes were large and filled with excitement.

"Yeah! Or, we could get tattoos!" It was also on her list, and if I had my choice of being stabbed by a needle one trillion times or jumping off of a skyscraper, I would choose the mutilation.

"No way!" Beck's mouth popped open, the light catching her lip gloss. I tried hard to keep my eyes on hers, but they kept dropping to her lips. Beck's expression shifted, and the window of opportunity for an epic night was closing fast. "Maybe we should wait until—"

"Let's order ourselves a cake and take it to the hot tub.

We can give everyone a little while longer to resurface, and if they don't, then we'll jump off a building by ourselves. Deal?" As I continued, Beck's lips sealed tight in deliberation. "We can't celebrate our birthdays without a cake. We need to make a wish, right?"

"Deal! You had me at cake . . ."

It wasn't my favorite plan, but at least she wasn't going back to her room alone to wait for her boyfriend. We didn't need to say goodbye to James. He wouldn't remember it tomorrow anyway. My eyes jumped from James to the Tethered Soul at the bar before leaving. He hadn't turned around, and I hoped that I would run into him again before the weekend was over.

CHAPTER 11

*B*eck dropped her towel on a nearby chair and kicked off her flip-flops. She reached her hand up to her hair and gathered it in a small ponytail and my eyes ran down her side, remembering our first time together. My jaw hardened, and my heart beat out of rhythm. Just as she lifted her head to look at me, I whipped my gaze away. Afraid I had given myself away, I made it worse by stumbling over my flip-flops. I looked back at her and caught the tail end of her smile. Of course, she saw it. I shook my head, disappointed in my lack of agility. I placed my card key on a small patio table before covering it with my towel, and then I pulled my shirt off over my head. If I wanted Beck to notice anything, it was this, but her back was turned.

I tried not to stare as Beck tiptoed into the hot tub. Her body was enveloped by the heat as steam rose around her. It was like a dream coming true before my very eyes, and I never wanted to wake up. My eyes trailed from her shoulders to her hips, noting the subtle differences from one life to the next. She was stronger. Healthier. Her skin, however, remained unchanged. Just as pale, it glistened like alabaster, even in the night's shadows.

"I really do want to bungee jump," she said, turning around to take me in. I was just as sun-deprived as she, but my skin didn't glisten with the multitude of undertones like hers. She was simply stunning.

I stepped into the water and the smell of chlorine permeated the air and burned my nostrils. Pins and needles pricked my toes as I stepped deeper. My eyes set on Beck.

"I just think I would feel so free . . . like a bird in flight. Do you think it feels like that?"

I couldn't help but let out a short, blunt laugh as I felt jumping would be the polar opposite. "No! I'm pretty sure it feels like your life is ending."

Beck splashed me in protest, and I flinched as the scalding water slapped at my chest. But I didn't think. I knew. I'd never bungee jumped before, but I had gone skydiving. And I related the freefall to anything but a bird in flight. "Birds are peaceful up there in the air. I think you've confused flying with falling."

Beck raised a brow. "Then why did you want to do it!?" she asked. It was a valid question. One I couldn't answer truthfully.

"I think it's good to do the things that scare you. It's what life's about, you know?"

Beck smiled softly and looked down into the water.

"Speaking of, I thought you were afraid of the water?" I

could see Beck blush even through the dim light and thick steam.

"Not when I can touch the bottom." Beck rolled her eyes. "It's so embarrassing. It's just this really weird irrational fear. I don't know what else to say about it."

"You don't have to say anything. Maybe you drowned in another lifetime or something?" I tested the waters and watched her intently for any show of recognition. And for a split second, I thought she seriously considered it. But then the air shifted, and I let the breath out that I hadn't known I was holding.

Beck laughed dismissively. "Oh, come on!" She rolled her eyes as if it were the stupidest thing she'd heard and picked up her cocktail and sucked down a substantial amount.

I wasn't ready to give up just yet. I waited, letting the thought simmer a while longer. Her eyebrows furrowed as she played with her straw. "How did we get here?" Beck asked as she swiped her hand across the rumbling bubbles of the water's surface, her eyes unfocused.

"What do you mean?" I asked.

"I mean, we're already twenty-one, and I don't know about you, but I have nothing figured out. Sometimes I feel like I don't even know who I am. I thought I would have a plan by now, you know? But I don't. Not even close. Do you ever just take a moment and reflect on your life, and wonder how the hell you got here? Do you ever wonder where you're going? Or what even matters in the first place?" Beck threw her head back and stared up at the stars.

I watched as the steam rose and collected under her chin. Her exposed throat begged to be kissed.

"You have no idea," I said, taking her drink from her and placing it on the hot tub's edge.

Beck looked at me, her eyes filled with sympathy, a shared understanding. "Sometimes I feel like my entire life has been a lie. I wonder if there's more out there. There has to be more to it than this."

She searched my eyes, desperately seeking understanding. "I worry more than I would like to admit that I'm living the wrong life," she said.

"The *wrong* life?"

"I mean, what if I took the wrong path? What if I get lost? It would be the wrong life. The one that wasn't meant for me."

"I know this may not seem like much coming from me, but I think you're living an extraordinary life," I said. I inched a little closer, fighting my instincts to comfort her.

"You do? What makes you think that?"

"Your heart runs so deep that I think you can make the impossible happen, and whoever you choose to open your heart to will be the luckiest soul to ever walk this earth." It poured out of me. No regrets.

Beck lifted one dripping hand and ran it through her hair. Her mouth partially separated as she bit into her bottom lip. And if I wasn't mistaken, I thought I saw a flash of hunger in her eyes.

"I wonder if our paths crossing a second time is a coincidence or something more. I feel something when I'm around you. Something I can't explain." Beck lowered deep into the water, her chin partially submerged and her eyes burrowing into me.

"Try?" I said.

"I couldn't even begin to explain it. And I'd be afraid of coming off like a complete lunatic. It's . . . I mean, it's . . ." Beck closed down and turned away from me. She moved to the opposite side of the Jacuzzi, one arm resting on the cold pavement as she looked into the distance.

"How about I tell you how I feel instead? I'll be the lunatic for both of us." I closed the distance between us and looked out into the darkness as she did.

Beck laughed nervously. "OK then . . . Give it your best shot."

"I feel like the stars have aligned ever so perfectly for our lives to intertwine . . . *again*." Beck brought her wet hands to her eyes, pressing her palms deep into her sockets. When her back rose with her heavy breath, I feared I had said too much. Too soon.

"Easton Green, *who are you*?" She cocked her head to the side and raised her eyebrows in question. It was more of an accusatory look than a warm invitation. My chest constricted and I swallowed down a bullet of worry. She knew I was more than a neighbor. That much was obvious, but the truth was still cloaked, and I feared it may scare her once she figured it out.

I closed my eyes and tilted my head up to the night sky. I didn't know what to say. *Who was I?* She was asking me, point-blank, and I couldn't answer. It was an impossible situation. In love with a girl who simply didn't remember me, and if she did, her entire world would crumble to her feet. It was in that moment that I wondered if I was better off not knowing her at all. If this would be slow torture, a new cage . . . another tether.

What she did next was the last thing I'd expected. Her body pressed against mine, and she wrapped her hand around the nape of my neck, pulling me down to her. I lowered my head as she lifted onto her toes, planting a wet chlorine kiss softly on my lips. I opened my eyes to see a flicker of desire reflect in her expression, and she was no longer Becca but my Everly Beck. She'd come home. I hated myself for ever thinking the pain wouldn't be worth it because in that moment, I knew I could chase her for all of eternity.

And then, without notice, as if awakened abruptly from a dream, her affection drained from her face and regret washed over her. "Oh my god, I'm *so* sorry! I don't know why I did that!"

"No, no, no. Don't be sorry!" I reached my hand out to grab her, but she was already stepping out of the hot tub. "Don't go, Beck!" I pleaded.

"I'm so sorry. I need to find Nolan!" Beck grabbed her towel and took off in a half walk, half jog, wrapping her towel tightly around her chest. In an instant, I was left with nothing more than her forgotten flip-flops and wet footprints on the pavement floor.

Three employees holding a small cake with a lit candle passed Beck on her way out. I closed my eyes, wishing them away, but when I opened them, they stood at the hot tub's edge. Two girls and one boy sang one of the worst renditions of "Happy Birthday" I'd ever heard. And that was saying a lot. Maybe it was the collective lack of talent, or maybe it was the pain of my broken heart boiling with the fear of losing my soulmate. But either way, it was one of the most difficult fifteen seconds I'd ever faked. When the coyote call was finally over, they held the cake out for me to make my wish. The candle danced wildly as if even it were protesting. I was so humiliated, I blew the candle out almost instantly, never making a wish at all. Which was a shame, because I could really use one.

"Where should we—" The three of them looked around for a place to put the birthday cake.

"You can just put it with my towel over there. Thank you," I said.

I didn't wait for them to leave. I took a deep breath and submerged myself to the bottom of the hot tub. The heat burned my cheeks, offering me temporary relief from the actual pain I felt inside. I knew now that the spark between Beck and I was not a fluke. The tether between her and I was still as strong as ever. Present, though her memory was not. And if I could hold on, just a little while longer, maybe she would come around.

I racked my brain, thinking of the possible ways I could help bring her memory back. I wondered how I could get her on the New River Bridge. How I could take her to the open field overlooking the Truly River and sit her in the roots of the dead oak tree. It wouldn't be a simple task, but it was a goal I could work towards. It was a goal I could focus on. Maybe then she'd come back to me.

An elderly couple approached the hot tub. The woman was holding onto her husband's arm for support as she took her first steps into the water. They smiled politely at me.

"Do you need a hand?" I asked.

"Oh, aren't you a sweetheart." The lady reached out and placed her small, frail hand in mine. I helped guide her down the steps as she yipped and yipped over how hot the water was.

"Well, what did you expect? It's called a hot tub for a reason, Marge!" The old man bickered.

I couldn't help but laugh, and through all the pain and suffering my heart had been through tonight, I couldn't help but find the humor in this geriatric couple. It was the blind leading the blind. They most likely had fallen into a rut where they only spoke to each other through jabs of criticism or sarcasm. And if I had to guess, they wouldn't have it any other way. I never wanted to grow old, but in that moment, I wanted nothing more than to grow old with Beck.

"You think you're so tough, why don't you come in here!"

"I'm coming! I'm coming! Someone's got to put your robe on the table! The Lord knows you won't do it." The man shuffled in his trunks to the water's surface.

"What's that?"

"Nothing!" The man grumbled as he stepped into the water. "Damn that's hot!"

"I *told* you!" The woman looked at me and shook her head exhaustedly.

"Yeah, it's a little hot, but it will feel good once you get used to it," I said.

The man froze, staring at me and patting his bare boobs. "Where are my glasses?" He looked between me and his wife.

It was the reason I never wanted to grow old before. I had no reason to wither away in body and soul if I had no one to do it with.

"They're on your head, you dummy!" She looked in my direction, and for the life of me, I couldn't figure out why I was included in the conversation. "I swear, he'd lose his own butt if it weren't attached!"

I chuckled, and the old man groaned as he took another step into the water. He waved his hand dismissively as if he'd heard it all before. I wondered what growing old with Beck would be like. And though I was worried I'd never have the chance to find out, I let myself hope. If I had made that wish, I would have wished for one long life with Beck.

"You two have a nice night," I said as I stepped out of the hot tub and grabbed my towel. Alone and deep in thought, I strolled back to my hotel room. But when I came to my room, I was shocked to see Payton slip out of Nolan's suite and stumble away, adjusting her clothing. She barreled down the hall, walking anything but straight. If she noticed me at all, she didn't say anything. I looked over my shoulder and watched her round the corner, twisting her ankle in her heels and nearly falling to the floor.

"God damn it!" she cursed, sharp enough for me to clearly hear it down the hallway. Her cutting tone was not from the pain of a twisted ankle but, rather, regret.

$\mathcal{I}$ pushed my door open and stepped inside my room, wondering where Beck had been, and if she had any knowledge of Payton's presence next door. I paced the depths of my hotel room in my towel until I couldn't take it any longer. After dressing in dry clothes, I headed to Brooklyn's room, hoping to find Beck. But when Brooklyn answered the door, I didn't see Beck wounded like I thought I might. Instead, I was surprised to see Payton there. If I had to guess, she was probably using Brooklyn as her alibi.

"Easton, come in. Have a drink."

"I'm just looking for Beck, have you seen her?"

"No. Payton, have you seen Beck?"

"Nope!" Payton said from inside.

"Come in!" Brooklyn echoed.

"Thanks, maybe later. See ya," I said, already making my getaway. Beck was nowhere in sight. And both girls appeared confused about where she might be. Only one of them was being honest, though.

I texted Beck, asking to talk, but she didn't reply. Tapping my phone across the palm of my hand, I stood beside the elevators, waiting for the reply that would never come. I took one last sweeping look for Beck down in the casino and bar before returning to my room for the night.

When the elevator door opened, a couple making out in the corner startled and separated. The man was wearing more of her lipstick than his partner. I joined them as they snickered behind my back. The elevator air was thick with anticipation—theirs and mine—but if we had to agree on one thing, it was that the elevator doors couldn't open soon enough. I closed my eyes and counted in my head until the electric buzz of people and machines crowded my senses.

Cigarette smoke clouded the floor, and the slots chimed obnoxiously. It was easy for one's senses to be overloaded. I tried to block it all out. Focus. I needed to hone in on my tether. But after walking a few laps around the casino and lobby, I found myself in the shadows of the hotel bar. Beck was nowhere to be found.

The redheaded soul sat hunched over the bar as if he hadn't moved an inch in the past decade. My shoulders dropped, letting go of the tension I'd been holding since Beck left me at the hot tub. Before opting to join the gentleman, I took one last peak—as far as my sight could travel. When Beck's ashen hair was nowhere to be found, I sat. The man's hair swept in front of his face, yet the hard lines of his jaw were still visibly tightened. He was like stone, petrified and historical.

"Two of whatever he's having, please," I said to the bartender.

I adjusted my barstool closer to the bar, and the gentleman ever so slowly turned to me. When he did, I could see the years of pain etched in his eyes. They were green with gold flecks. He was an Irishman. Middle-aged on the outside, but his soul reached well beyond the time I'd seen. He studied me, as I did him. I waited for him to speak first. Perhaps he didn't want to talk at all. Either way, I'd be here to let him know he wasn't alone. Even if it were for just a drink.

The bartender placed two whiskey and sevens in front of us, and I handed him my credit card and ID.

The bartender looked at my ID and smiled. "Happy Birthday, man!"

"Thank you."

The Irishmen slid his empty glass to the bartender, who took it with an exasperated glint in his eyes. He'd probably been here longer than this evening alone. Maybe days or a week.

"Huh," he grunted after sipping his refreshed whiskey. "I haven't come across one of you for a long time."

"Few and far between," I nodded, slugging back a gulp. The amber liquid lashed out, burning my chest and settling in my belly.

"They sure are." He held his glass up to cheers mine. The glasses clinked together, and I slapped his back before finishing my double shot.

"Do you have time for a story?" I asked. His need for camaraderie was nearly tangible, but he was slow to open up. He reminded me of Clyde in this way, which made me like him even more. I knew *my* story would breathe life back into him. He didn't speak, but instead, turned his focus to me. I told him all about Beck. Her cancer. Our crash. Finally, her forgotten love. I'd lost all sense of time. One drink after another, and I could have talked for hours. Probably did. I thought he almost didn't believe it, but by the time I finished speaking, I could see that he did. His jaw had slackened, and his eyes took on a softer tone. He not only believed me, but he was moved by my story.

"She's here?" he asked, peering around the bar.

"Yeah. Somewhere."

"Damn. I'd never heard such a story." He shook his head. An unheard story was hard to come by when you'd been around as long as we had.

"Me neither! I was hoping you'd have some advice for me!" I took a deep swig of my drink. It was most likely the one that put me over the edge.

He laughed, "Me? Oh, no, no, no. Just because I've seen a lot, doesn't give me the right to hand out advice. Lord knows I've made a muck of my own lives." He shook his head and took down the last of his drink, proceeding to watch his ice in the bottom of his glass as he swirled his tumbler around in small circles.

"I guess you need more practice." I laughed under my breath, and the stone man found the humor too. His hunched back bounced before his face fell flat once more.

"Yes, fella. That's surely what I need. But if I know one thing, it's not in the cards." He stood up and threw his jacket over his shoulder. He was a tall man, much taller than I expected. "Now, I don't do this regularly, and I have half the mind to tell you not to listen to me. But I'm going to leave you with a bit to chew on."

"Alright then." I swiveled in my barstool and clasped my hands in my lap awaiting the Irish advice from a man who hadn't yet figured out his own life. Despite the many tries.

"Tell her the truth," he said, blunt and harsh—true to fashion.

It hit harder than I'd imagined it would. The word *truth,* burning a hole in my stomach far worse than the whiskey. As if I'd been the one hiding it from her. I never wanted to hide anything from her.

The man placed his gigantic hand on my shoulder and squeezed. "Take care of yourself."

I nodded.

He was halfway out of the bar when I yelled after him, "Hey, I didn't catch your name!"

"William!" He waved over his head as he disappeared around the corner.

I woke abruptly that morning with a text from Brooklyn. The ping pounded in my head, nearly rupturing my temples.

Meet at the buffet for breakfast in ten.

I jumped to my feet, grasping at my temples. *Water.* I needed water. I opened up the mini-fridge and grabbed an overpriced water. Ripping the cap off, I guzzled it down. I brushed my teeth as I dressed one-handed. I barely had my shoes on by the time the hotel door slammed behind me. Beck's room was quiet, and despite checking my phone a million times over, she had not texted, and I wondered if she would be at breakfast.

I wasn't hungry until I caught the smell of bacon and syrup wafting in the air as I neared the breakfast buffet. I immediately spotted Brooklyn and Payton at a table near the entry. I sat down next to Brooklyn and across from Payton, who repelled my eye contact.

"Morning! How was your night last night? Did you ever find Becca?" Brooklyn asked.

"No, I didn't. She never stopped by your room?"

Brooklyn shook her head but then lifted her gaze and said, "Speak of the devil!"

I whipped around to see Beck, her face pale and puffy. She too avoided eye contact. Nolan was quick on her heels, and he had a distinct air to him. If there were a word for his aura. I'd say . . . *smug*.

Nolan took the seat furthest away from me, leaving only two options for Beck to choose from. She opted to sit between Nolan and Payton. *That's* how much distaste she had for me?

"Where's James?" I asked.

Payton laughed, "You'll be lucky if you see James before the plane ride home." When our eyes met, there wasn't an ounce of guilt behind them. I couldn't tell if it was because she wasn't sorry or she thought she hadn't gotten caught.

Nolan let out a muffled huff and added, "*If* he makes the plane."

Everyone seemed to agree it was a real possibility that James would be stuck here in Sin City. I gathered it was for no reason other than his lack of responsibility and short-sightedness. From what I saw last night in the bar, I was sure that he could be easily sidetracked by anyone who gave him their undivided attention.

Our server approached with a full pot of coffee, and my stomach turned sour at the sight alone. After our coffees were poured, our table was released to the madness of the buffet. Everyone split, and I took special notice that Beck started in the opposite direction of Nolan. Had she seen what I saw last night? Did she suspect Nolan was with Payton? Perhaps the most important question was, did it matter?

I took a clean plate into my hands and snuck behind her at the fruit and yogurt bar.

"You're avoiding me . . ." I saw no point in beating around the bush when I had so little time to talk to her. It wouldn't be long before we were in earshot of one of her friends. And in a matter of seconds, she could be at the omelet station, and I'd be standing in the middle of the bustling buffet . . . with Nolan.

"No!" Beck said in a sharp tone.

"Yes, you are. Strawberries?" I held a spoonful of strawberries between us and she paused, softening a little before moving her plate underneath the spoon. Ripe red strawberries rolled across her plate.

"OK! I am. It's awkward! And I'm sorry about last night. I feel like an ass. It's just, it shouldn't have happened," Beck admitted.

It was a blow but not an unexpected one. I'd already had the night to feed upon her regrets. I pushed them aside and trudged forward. "Beck, we're friends, right?" I'd used this a time or two on her before, and it worked well. There was no reason to think it wouldn't now.

"Um, yeah. Sure."

Unconvincing. I furrowed my brows. "Whipped cream?"

"Yes, please," she said. Interesting, how she was so sure she wanted whipped cream on her strawberries but not so sure that her neighbor from when she was eight—her two times over husband, her soulmate—was worthy of such a simple title as *friend.* I slopped the whipped cream on top of her fruit, and it was the glue that held the berries together.

"Don't think for one second that our *friendship* is so easily disposable. If you want to forget this kiss, it's as good as forgotten," I said, hushed.

Beck stopped and looked up to meet my eyes for the first time since our kiss in the hot tub. And in lieu of a response, she nodded.

Just because lying was so easy for me, it didn't make it acceptable. William's advice rang through my head. I knew that deceit was wrong. But it came with the territory. And if Beck was more comfortable thinking I'd forgotten last night's kiss, then so be it. The truth was, I was like an elephant. Every detail of all my lives was preciously preserved in my memory. Except for the first few lives, that is. They were . . . fuzzy. I presumed this is how Beck's memory would work as well. In a couple more lifetimes, she wouldn't remember I had lied to her. And my highest hopes were that she wouldn't remember a time when her love for me fell absent.

Our group ate breakfast while rehashing the night before. Trying to figure out how each puzzle piece fit together—the when's and how's of how everyone ended up separated. I caught a few stolen glances between Nolan and Payton while Beck moved her food around on her plate absentmindedly. James showed halfway through breakfast somewhere between our first and second helpings of unlimited food.

"James! You're alive! I was beginning to worry!" Payton called out.

"No, you weren't!" James said.

"You're right, I wasn't!" Payton laughed.

James approached our table, and his hungry eyes scanned the massacre of dishes and uneaten food on the table. He grabbed Nolan's shoulder and squeezed it tight, intending to inflict as much pain as possible, but Nolan was nearly twice his size. "Oh, man! You're eating Polish sausage? That's a *bold* move!"

Nolan pulled away from James's grip. "No! It's good! You should try it!"

My stomach turned at the very sight of his sausage link. Mixed splotches of brown and grey. Three down, one left to go.

"I'm all good! I think I'll pass on the water-rhea!" James took off in search of food as the table chuckled in his wake.

The chatter continued in James's absence, but when he returned with his breakfast, the conversation took on a whole new life. It was crude and brash, and I loved every moment. Shots flew in every direction. Some aimed at my hair, some fired toward James's sex-capades from the night before, but most . . . Most were aimed towards Nolan and his grumbling stomach.

He tried to play it cool, but when his knuckles turned white, and sweat beaded at his hairline, I about rolled out of my chair laughing. I wanted desperately to control the sound that exploded from our table, but I couldn't think about the other guests' dining experience with that ferocious rumbling coming from the depths of Nolan's intestines. No, all I could think about was air! I needed to breathe but couldn't! My head was nearly resting on the table, I was so doubled over, and tears streamed from my eyes. All of my worries had been chased away by laughter. Every time I thought I had a handle on it, Nolan's stomach would grumble again, and the group would erupt into a fit of laughter. Even Beck. *Especially* Beck.

Finally, when Nolan couldn't play tough anymore, he slammed his fist down on the table and said, "Screw this!" and stormed off. Through teary eyes, I could just make out Nolan trotting off, tail tucked as he ran straight to one of the nearest restrooms.

It was the best thing I'd seen in years, and I wished I hadn't eaten so much because my stomach was taking a beating from laughter. There was no doubt in my mind about having pulled at least one abdominal muscle. Brooklyn rubbed her eyes so viciously, mascara ran down her cheeks, making her look like a panda bear. Beck wiped away the tears from her swollen eyes. If she enjoyed it more than she should have—and I think she did—I knew why. She must have had her suspicions about Nolan's loyalty.

By the time breakfast was over, I had a new fondness for Beck's friends. James and his endless stream of dialogue were truly a brightly burning candle. One day, I imagined I'd miss having him around. And when the dust settled, Brooklyn put eye drops into her eyes, the excess streaming down her mascara-stained cheeks, before winking at me with a marked sense of pride.

CHAPTER 13

With breakfast over, the group retreated to their rooms. I lingered. It was an invitation for Beck to pick up where we'd left off, and it didn't go unnoticed. She turned, playing with the sleeves of her shirt. Only after she opened her mouth did she close it again and stare at her shoes. She didn't have to say anything to express herself. I could feel it in the surrounding air. Her worry collided with anticipation and burst into a plume of wonder. It was enough to make my heart swell. At the very least, she wasn't mad at me.

"What are you going to do today? It's your last day in Sin City, and your boyfriend has food poisoning," I said.

"He's *not* my boyfriend!" Beck's face filled with distaste.

Surprise washed over me. "Wait, he's not?"

Beck's eyes scanned the casino, looking for answers in the flashing lights, and when she found what she was looking for, she said, "Come on!" She grabbed my arm, pulling me to her side.

"Where are we going?"

"We have living to do!"

A snort escaped me. "And what does that mean, specifically?"

"We're going bungee jumping!"

I was thankful she didn't turn around to see my face when she said it. If she had, she would have witnessed an awful shade of green in my cheeks. My gait slowed naturally as I instinctively tried to postpone the leap. But she only tightened her grip and charged forward. Sometimes the girl knew just what she wanted. Who was I to get in the way? I swallowed the sour taste of fear and told myself to suck it up. I had to be brave for Beck, and that's precisely what I intended to do. I had the entire trip to the launch pad to get myself there.

I caught up to her, side by side, and scanned her expression. It was cold, her eyes vacant. She didn't want to live. She just had something to prove. My guess was that it had to do with Nolan. But if she wanted to prove to herself that she didn't need him to have a memorable twenty-first birthday. Who was I to judge? I loved her either way, and I'd be jumping off the tallest skyscraper in the state to prove it to her.

"You're sure you want to do this?" I asked, my long legs in stride to keep up with her pace.

"Absolutely!" She continued, her sights set on hailing a taxi.

Beck didn't glance in my direction until we were inside the cab, and even then, it was brief. She looked away the second I returned her attention. I knew she was hurting inside, and I wanted desperately to take that away for her, but it was hard to do when she refused to let me in. I pulled my gaze away from the back of her head and stared out my window.

It was a short distance to the destination, but the traffic caused the ride to be much longer than expected. When we arrived, I tipped the cab driver and helped Beck out of the car. She placed her hand in mine, and I gripped it tight, not wanting to let go. She pulled her hand back when she was upright, and I couldn't help the wash of disappointment that spread through my chest.

"Do you want to talk about—"

"About what?" Beck asked in a tone that was intended to be light and airy but only sounded disingenuous.

I nodded, taking the hint that now was not the time for her innermost confessions. Perhaps it would have to wait until after we lost our breakfast.

We signed up for the jump and were thrust into a twenty-minute educational course. They taught us what to expect, what to do, and what not to do. Beck's focus was intense, but I mainly paid attention to her. Dying would be a bitch, but it didn't hold as much weight for me as it did everyone else. I thought back to William, the Irishman, and imagined he would jump without even taking the safety course. Me, on the other hand, I'd just let the lesson float in one ear and out the other while I dreamed about my wife.

The time had come for our jump, despite my efforts to stop time altogether. The elevator filled with tension so thick that Beck was having trouble keeping her breathing under control. Her face flushed, and her hands were restless at her side. I couldn't help but smile.

"What? Don't give me that look!"

"You're really scared, aren't you?" I asked.

"No, I'm not!"

I stared at her in disbelief and called her out on her bluff. "Liar!"

A sharp *bing* signified we were at the top of the skyscraper, and Beck jumped a fitting mile high. I bit my cheek as Beck's body betrayed her. The elevator doors opened, and I tried my damnedest to hold it in, but I was busting at the seams. A loud boisterous laugh escaped me and I covered my mouth with not one but both hands. The angrier Beck got, the harder I laughed. I could hardly hear anything the guy said when he was binding my feet. Tears welled up in my eyes, and I clutched my stomach. It was breakfast all over again as my nerves transformed into hysteria.

"Stop that!" Beck hissed as her feet were being bound. The smallest curvature of her lips told me that in some small way, I was helping to distract her. It wasn't on purpose, though. I couldn't help the fact that she pretended to be so confident, but when the time had come, she was crumbling to pieces. It was *so* Beck.

The two men helped Beck and me to our feet, and gave us one last rundown of instructions before walking us out to the edge of the building. Beck and I stood on two red Xs in front of an endless panoramic view. The air was cool and the sky cloudless. The world bustled below, unaware of our pounding hearts above. I looked down at the congestion of traffic below, and I couldn't help feeling relieved being so far removed from it all. If I wasn't about to plunge eight hundred feet down, I might see how this would remind Beck of a bird in flight.

Triple checks were being made on our safety before we were told to walk to the edge. I smiled at Beck, but my face fell flat when I saw she was not having the same experience as I was. Her face was pale as a ghost, and her eyes the size of golf balls.

"Hey, Beck. Look at me!" Ever so slowly she turned her head, and our eyes locked. "You are an incredibly strong woman. You don't need Nolan or anyone else for that matter. You've got this!" Beck puckered her lips and blew out a breath she'd been holding tight. "We're going to do this together, OK? You wanted to live, and this was on your list. Right here, right now, you're going to check this off! You're going to be a bird, and it's going to be just like you're flying! You still want to fly right?"

Beck nodded slowly, tears forming in her eyes.

"OK, I'll be right there with you. I promise, Beck. I'll be right by your side! Do you trust me?"

Beck sucked in a breath and nodded once more. Her hands were balled into white fists at her sides.

"Alright, I'm going to count to three, and you're going to tip forward. On my count! One!"

A small squeal escaped Beck's throat.

". . . Two!"

"Fuck, fuck, fuck, fuck," Beck said under her breath. I curled my toes in my shoes and felt the ledge give way underneath them. Suddenly I was back on the New River Bridge on the cold, wet night that I met Beck.

"Three! Go!"

Shit! I closed my eyes and let my body fall forward. Gravity sucked me into its vortex as I plunged downward. Time sped and slowed to a crawl, all at the same moment. Beck let out a guttural scream that slipped into the distance between us. The freefall was one I'd felt before and similar to what I would have felt if I had jumped off the New River Bridge. I braced myself for the darkness. The darkness that only followed death. In the moment, bursting with adrenaline, I'd forgotten that I would open my eyes once the fall was over.

This jump was made for the thrill. Coming close to death but not yet touching it. It wasn't a thrill to me—to someone who had died a dozen times too many. And no matter how many times I might take a jump like this, my life would start over again. And again.

I was lost in the moment of falling. Wrapped up in the feeling of dying—without death—that I didn't realize something was wrong. Off. Beck's scream was not by my side. And when I heard it, the feral sound stretched until it was gaping between us.

I opened my eyes to see the world spinning and tumbling. I flailed around, trying to get an understanding of the world as I knew it. The tension on the bungee reached its max capacity and recoiled like a rubber band. Blood rushed to my head and my feet pulled before I was falling in reverse. This was an entirely new feeling and one

I liked even less. But it was on my up that I could see that Beck's bungee had never left the platform.

My speed slowed until I was nearly floating in midair. Then the fall came again. And again. And again. When the torture was finally over, I hung upside down, suspended from the skyscraper, my eyes wanting to bulge from my head as the pressure built. My arms outstretched overhead, and I swung slightly as they pulled me up. All I could think was, *She didn't jump*. I couldn't believe she didn't jump! Beck didn't know it yet, but she was my partner. We didn't have one lifetime together but an infinite amount of time on this earth. Had she known that, I'm confident, she would have jumped. But because she didn't, I'd spend the rest of my life getting her back.

When I breached the platform, and my body was finally resting upright, my head spun. I could feel the blood funneling down to my extremities. Chasing away the pins and needles. When my vision finally cleared, I turned to look at Beck, who hadn't spoken a single word. Her eyes were huge, her hands cupping her mouth. A small squeak sounded but nothing comprehensible. We stared at each other while the men untied my legs.

"I thought we had living to do?" I cocked my head to the side.

"I'm so sorry!" Beck finally said.

"It's OK. It's my fault. When I said, I'd be by your side, I assumed, that went both ways. But I was mistaken," I said, shaking my head and pretending not to care. But the truth was, I was *so* going to get her back!

"I'm seriously so sorry! I couldn't do it!" Beck grabbed her stomach, still shaken.

I scrambled to my feet, a little unsteady, and held my arms out for a hug. She came bounding into my arms, and I wrapped them around her tight. The smell of coconut brought me back to a time when I was tangled up with her in bedsheets. I wanted to live in the memory but forced myself back to the present. Another nervous man was being strapped and lectured. He peered at me nervously.

"It's OK, really. But you owe me," I said with a smile.

Beck laughed a wildly nervous laugh. "Deal!" she said. Her breath was warm against my neck, and I didn't want to let her go.

She pulled away. "How was it? Tell me everything!" Beck asked as we walked to a nearby lookout point. The same magnificent view but with the safety of guardrails and plexiglass.

"It was amazing . . . really like spreading your wings and flying," I said.

Beck tipped her head back and laughed out loud. I joined her and shook my head. "Honestly, though, the worst part was opening my eyes and seeing that you weren't by my side."

Beck's laughter fizzled out and her eyes glistened. The air began to shift between us, and I could feel her coming back to me. Her face regained some color, and her cheeks turned pink.

"I'm sorry about last night," Beck said, looking at her feet.

"About leaving me in the hot tub? You know I had to

listen to the world's worst rendition of Happy Birthday all by my lonesome, right? And then I gave our cake to an old grumpy couple. I didn't even get to make a wish."

"About the kiss." Beck corrected me.

"Oh?"

"I shouldn't have kissed you. I think I just drank too much. Got swept away." Beck waved her hand in the air dismissively.

And if I looked just deep enough, through the hurt of her cutting words, through the fear of losing her again, I could see it. She was saying what she thought she needed to say in order to protect herself. I remembered a time when she admitted to having a nasty habit of destroying her chances at happiness. She was her own worst enemy. The hand that held her down.

"Well, I sometimes do that to women."

Beck snorted, and unfortunately, we both knew I was being sarcastic.

"You know, it's like I feel this weird connection with you. I feel so . . . so *grounded*. Is that a thing? I don't know. I just don't want to jeopardize that with something as stupid as Nolan drama. You were my best friend. And I'd like it if we went back to that," Beck said.

I could see right through her. The shift in her eyes. Her posture. She was afraid of the feelings she had inside. Perhaps the memories too? So, she was building a wall. Brick by brick.

"Can I ask you something?"

Beck stared out at the cars below. "Anything." Her tone was warm and inviting.

"Did you want to jump?"

Beck looked at me, eyebrows knitted. At first, it appeared that she thought the question was simple. Stupid even. But then, when she really thought about it, her thoughts delved deeper and deeper. "I did. I wanted to," she said so in question.

"So, why didn't you?"

Beck wasn't surprised by this question. She knew it was the difficult part that followed her first answer. She wanted to, but something stopped her. *She* stopped her. But why? Why would anyone get in their own way?

"I was afraid."

"Afraid of what, though?" I asked.

"I don't know. Of dying!" Beck shifted uncomfortably. It was my cue not to lay off but to push further. Dig deeper.

"Did you really think you were going to die if you jumped?" I asked.

Beck's cheeks turned pink. Her hand raised, then fell aimlessly. "I don't know. What do you want me to say?" Her voice rose in frequency.

"I just want you to be honest with yourself. That's all. It would be nice if you were honest with me too." I mumbled the last part.

Beck thrust a hand on her hip and huffed out a sharp breath. I stood still, watching the world below. Then I took a step onto the bottom rail.

"What are you doing!" Beck hissed, looking over her shoulder.

I rested my forehead on the plexiglass and slowly lifted

my hands away. The view was almost as clear as standing on the launch pad before jumping. "Join me."

It took a moment, but Beck did. I reached for her hand and pulled it away from the glass. She whimpered, but this time, I didn't let go. When her breathing gave way to slow and even breaths, I could see the thrill in her smile.

"Wow," she said, turning as much as she could to look at me as our foreheads pressed against the window and our hands locked tight at our sides.

"Hey! You can't be up there!" A security guard yelled.

Beck squeaked, and we both made a mad dash to jump off the rail. We awarded ourselves an escort down the one-hundred-and-three-story elevator. Snickering all the way down. And nothing in this world felt better than when I looked into her green eyes, and I knew the smile on her face was there because of me.

CHAPTER 14

The day warmed as the sun crawled high in the sky. Traffic moved all around us while Beck and I stood still. She was lost. She was away on a birthday weekend that had turned out to be nothing like what she planned. I wondered what her weekend would have looked like if I hadn't tagged along. Perhaps Nolan wouldn't have found himself alone with Payton. I couldn't help but feel responsible for the turn of events. I needed to make it up to Beck. Make sure she had an unforgettable trip.

"So, you've always wanted to bungee jump, but"—I shook my head and sighed—"what else have you always wanted to do? Maybe there's still time," I said, checking my watch.

Beck rolled her eyes. "You're never going to let me live that one down, are you?"

"Nope!"

Beck accepted her fate with a heavy sigh. Then a look I was beginning to recognize crept across her face. "I should get that tattoo. Yeah, I should totally get a tattoo!" Beck said, eyes widening in excitement.

"Then you should! Let's do it!" I said.

"You're going to get one too, right?" Beck asked.

Me? I'd had my share of tattoos. In one life, I was covered with them. Not just from arm to arm but everywhere. They'd become addictive. The art was beautiful when fresh. Until it wasn't. Until I wanted something different. When the time came, I wanted to express myself differently and couldn't. It's true that I enjoyed them, but I also never had one I didn't regret at one time or another. "This one's all you . . ."

"Oh, come on, you baby!" said Beck in a playful tone, shoving my arm.

"Oh! I'm the baby?" I stopped walking and slowly raised my finger to point at the now distant skyscraper that I'd leapt off, while she stayed permanently affixed to the surface in safety.

"OK! OK! I take it back! Please, let it go! You're not a baby."

I remained frozen, pointing, unsatisfied.

"You're . . . brave!" Beck pled.

As soon as she said it, I only hungered for more. "And?"

"And . . . adventurous!" Beck said.

"And?" I prodded. Beck tilted her head in protest, but I encouraged her to keep going with a wave of my hand.

"And . . . spirited, kind, um . . . attractive . . . kind of . . ."

My accusatory pointer finger fell from the skyscraper, and I closed the distance between us. She stood her ground when I lowered down to her. Slowly. Slowly enough to gauge if she would let me kiss her. If her eye contact told me anything, it was that she was open to the idea of another kiss. One that was sober and in the open daylight of clear cognitive thought and emotions. I brought my lips close to hers before brushing by them. Trailing my lips against her cheek, making my way to her ear. Then I whispered, *"Kind* of?"

Beck let out the breath she'd been holding in, and I couldn't contain the smile that pulled across my face. The tension, having peaked, came crashing down around us. Beck took her frustration out on me, wailing on me two palms at a time as I flinched away and laughed at her. This was going to be fun. I liked this Beck. The one that didn't have impending doom on the edge of her heart. The one who fought back.

"You! Little! Errrr!"

I hailed a taxi as Beck stole little glances at me from behind the curtain of her hair. I pretended not to notice, but it wasn't any good with the foolish grin I had plastered on my face. I couldn't for the life of me hide how I was feeling inside. We had that in common. But by the time we pulled up to the tattoo parlor, it was clear that Beck was feeling something else entirely.

"Are you sure about this?" I asked.

"Yeah!" Beck squeaked.

I'd heard that confidence not too long ago. "You know, because it's not too late to fail at this, too," I said and smiled.

"Stop! I'm going to do it!" Beck said, convincing herself more than me.

We walked into the parlor, and the buzz of a tattoo gun was the first thing that brought me back to the hours I'd spent in the chair. Drawings covered the walls and the man who greeted us alike.

"Can I help you?" the man asked. His thin frame covered in colorful ink and large studs adorned his ears.

"Hi, um, this one was thinking about getting a tattoo today. Do you have availability for a walk-in?" I asked, not staring at the man himself or his tattoos but my reflection on his shaved head.

The man looked at his watch. "I guess it depends on what you want. I have an appointment at 3:00, and I can squeeze you in if it's simple enough. Do you know what you want?" The man looked between Beck and me.

"I do. And yes, it's simple," Beck said.

I was surprised that she already knew what she wanted. She'd put some thought into this before. I wondered what she valued enough that she would display it on her body for years to come. I hoped whatever she chose wouldn't be a part of the lie she'd grown up believing. Because then, I'd feel obligated to speak up.

"Then let's do this. I'm Zack, and I'll get some paperwork for you. You can fill it out while I draw you up a sketch and get the quote ready. What is it you wanted to get?"

I looked down at Beck, curious. "I wanted to get an infinity symbol. Right here." Beck pointed to her side. My heart just about dropped into my stomach. The girl remembered more than she led on.

"Why?" I mumbled under my breath. Barely audible.

Beck peeped at me before accepting the paperwork from her soon-to-be tattoo artist and filled out her information.

"Why?" I asked again, slightly louder.

Beck stopped writing and looked up at me, "Why what?"

"Why that?"

Beck shrugged. I thought something profound would come next. A clue, perhaps. Or a memory that she made into a dream. But when she said, "I don't know. I like it!" I had to second guess if it was a sign at all. Maybe I was trying to will a memory that simply wasn't there. Did she like it in how girls liked to draw hearts? Or did she like it in the way that resonated with her on a deep and meaningful level?

I watched Beck make a small x on the human body drawing of her paperwork. She wanted her infinity symbol on the side of her ribs in a place that I imagined her bra would cover. Hidden, intimate. I waited on a bench while she approved the sketch and paid the cashier. When the artist was ready, I moved a chair to be by her side.

Beck removed her bra and blushed a bright crimson as she shoved her sexy undergarment in her purse. She lay down on the chair and lifted her shirt high, struggling to keep her chest hidden and get comfortable at the same time. My eyes trailed down her ribcage, and my heart quickened.

"I need you to rest your arm over your head like this." Zack held his arm against his ear, and Beck imitated him. She looked at me while he wiped down her skin. Tiny goosebumps pimpled her side, and worry pricked the corners of her eyes.

"Hold my hand?" Beck asked.

I rolled my chair closer to her, took her hand in mine, and held it tight, stroking her knuckles with my thumb. "You've got this. Why don't you tell me why you choose the infinity symbol? Other than just liking it. There's got to be more to it than that."

Zack tested his gun, and Beck flinched at the sound.

"It's OK, honey. I'm not starting yet. I'll let you know first," he said.

Beck nodded, embarrassed, before she turned her attention back to me. "Um, I think that sometimes . . ." She looked back down at the gun and struggled to focus. But I needed her to. I needed her to focus on what she was telling me. "I think that, there are things in this world that . . ." Her eyes dropped once again.

"OK, honey. We're going to start. Just a light pricking feeling. Try not to jump."

"In this world that, what Beck?" I asked.

"That never truly—"

The gun pierced her skin and Beck yelped, jumping two feet into the air. Zack pulled his gun back and yelled, "Fuck!"

"Nope!" Beck leaped off of the bed. "Nope. I can't! I can't do it!" Beck became unglued, her eyes fear-stricken and her body tremulous.

I didn't have to ask if she was sure. I knew. Everyone knew. I looked back to Zack, whose mouth still gaped open, the gun still lifted into the air. "We're going to take an intermission. But if she finds the courage to come back and finish—which she won't—we'll call and make an appointment first. I'll get your card on the way out," I said. Beck was already halfway out of the parlor, and the door was swinging closed behind her.

"Sorry, man. I told her not to move! She's going to have to come back to get that fixed!" Zack said.

"Oh, no. Don't worry. Yeah, I'll get her to come back. It might just take a little time is all!" I lied. I knew we were on a flight out first thing tomorrow morning. And I knew by the look on Beck's face that she wouldn't give this a second chance.

As I walked out of the parlor, I couldn't help but remember taking Beck to crash a wedding. She was absolutely horrified. And when I brought her camping, it was no different. I didn't bother taking the man's business card on the way out. I was too deep in thought. What made this girl so afraid of what she really wanted? I found Beck pacing the parking lot. I grabbed her tight, pulling her into my embrace. She trembled against my body and sobbed. "Shhh."

"I'm so embarrassed!" Beck said when she had settled enough.

"Shhh, it's OK." I stroked the back of her head and pondered over what was holding her back. But perhaps the most important question wasn't what was holding her back, but what propelled one forward. "I thought you wanted to get a tattoo. It was on your list!" I said.

"My list? Why do you keep saying that?" Beck pulled away. Her eyes red and laced with confusion.

Shit. "I mean, you said you'd always wanted to get one." I looked away and hoped the moment would pass.

"I did! I thought I did. I don't know what's wrong with me! I have this bad habit of self-destruction. It's like I get so close to the thing I want, and then I find a way to destroy it," Beck echoed. I remembered her saying it two decades ago. It would not be an easy fix, but we had the time to work on it. I wanted that for her.

"Well, let's take a look and see what you got," I said as I reached out for the hem of Beck's top. She helped guide her shirt up to her ribcage. My brows peeked, and I hid my mouth behind my hand.

"What? Is it bad?" Beck asked, unable to see.

I tried to tell her it wasn't. I tried! But it just came out as full-blown manic laughter that busted the seams of my cupped fingers. What I saw could only be described as a . . . comma. A comma that was made by a passenger in flight. One that hit turbulence.

"Oh my god, Easton! Is it that bad?" Beck tried to manipulate her body. Bend and fold in every which way to see it. She couldn't. I spun around to gather myself but ultimately folded in half, bracing my hands on my knees. I wanted to get Beck back for making me jump off the skyscraper alone, but the poor girl just couldn't help doing it to herself. And I couldn't help but laugh at her mishaps. I'd probably laughed more in the last two days than I had throughout the whole of this very life. I prayed Beck would never grow out of it. Because her lack of grace might have been my favorite thing about her.

"What the hell is that?!" Beck squawked as she held her cell phone out to her side.

"Congratulations! It's a twig!" I said. Beck lifted her head, but her jaw remained on the floor.

Beck and I finished the day at the drug store, getting her a salve and bandage for her skewed comma tattoo before heading back to the hotel. She didn't seem overly concerned about checking on Nolan, and I didn't blame her. I'd had the best day with her. It was epic, really. And I took pleasure in knowing that every time she would see the ink on her bare body, she'd think of me. Maybe not favorably, as I did laugh pretty hard at her in the parking lot, but all the same, she'd think of me.

That night I could hear her and Nolan fighting from across the hall. His tone was loud and accusatory. Hers high-pitched and sharp. And I couldn't imagine a situation in which I felt so helpless. I sat with my back against the front door of my room and listened to the rise and fall of their argument. I couldn't make out what they were yelling, but I guessed it either had to do with Payton or me. Perhaps both.

I wanted them to break up but not like this. Not with pain. I never wanted that for Beck. I ran my hands through my hair, wishing it all away. Dreaming of a time when Beck and I were together again and there were no more secrets. And no more Nolans.

Irishman William's advice rung vividly in my head. Neither qualified nor founded but still solid. I weighed the possibilities of telling Beck the truth. Her past life, who I really was, and what it really meant to be a Tethered Soul. And had I not had so much to lose, it might be worth it. But for now, when I still had the smallest chance to be with her, I had to hold off. Save it for a time when there was no going back, and I was all out of hope. There *would* be a time. *That* I was sure of, but the time was not now. I steepled my fingers under my chin, thinking about how afraid she was to jump. I couldn't imagine what learning of her immortality might do to her.

Having grown tired of listening to the muffled dispute between Beck and Nolan, I opened my door and slid the lock in between the door jamb. I hoped that Beck would see it as an invitation if she didn't want to stay the night with Nolan after their fight. I left the bathroom light on for her and crawled into bed. I closed my eyes, exhausted from the emotional distress of the weekend, and drifted off to sleep.

CHAPTER 15

$\mathcal{I}$t was some time into the night when I dreamed of Beck. Her warm body against mine. The scent of coconut-infused hair curling around me like a vice. So real I questioned if I was asleep at all. When my dream slipped away and Beck remained tangled in my arms, my mind raced to gather the fragmented pieces. My eyes fluttered as I looked around the darkness of the room, and I remembered I'd left the door open for Beck. The small light peeking out from the bathroom cast a warm glow on her cheekbone and illuminated her resting eyes.

I thought long and hard about what she needed in that moment, and as much as I wanted to close the distance between her lips and mine, I knew she was a lifetime behind me. Unlike me, who held my spouse in bed, she was lying with a friend. A neighbor.

A single teardrop fell upon my hand. I squeezed her a little tighter but said nothing. Sometimes, pain just needed to be felt. And it helped to have someone by your side. This wasn't the time for questions. I knew that much. I nestled my forehead into the back of her head and tried my damn hardest to go anywhere but the field of wet grass on the day we wed.

I woke before my alarm went off. It was hard not to with Beck on my arm. Like waking up to gifts early Christmas morning, I was too excited for sleep. I watched her eyes twitch in the early morning light before attempting to withdraw my arm. She rolled off of it, still sound asleep. Once free, I padded barefoot to the restroom. As quietly as I could, I began packing for the airport. I knew Beck would have to do the same, but I dreaded waking her up and sending her back to Nolan's room to pack her belongings. It hardly seemed fair.

My ears perked when I heard a faint vibration. I opened the bathroom door to hear the sound magnify and Beck stirring in bed. Her phone rested on top of her bag, and I nearly tripped over her suitcase in my pursuit of it. *Smart girl.* She must have packed last night. I grasped her phone to silence it but not before seeing the dozens of text messages left unread by Nolan. My eyes landed on words like *fault*, and *Easton*.

"Was that my phone? What time is it?" Beck murmured.

I spun around with her phone in my hand, trying not to look suspicious. "Sorry, I was just trying to silence it. Are you OK?" I asked.

Beck ran her hands through her tangled hair and

squinted into the light. She said nothing. I brought her the phone and sat at the foot of the bed while she paged through her texts. A moment later, she tossed her phone onto the fluff of the hotel comforter, shaking her head.

"Nolan hooked up with Payton," Beck said.

"I'm sorry."

"He thinks I have a thing for you. He said it was my fault," Beck said, watching her fingers intertwine.

I swallowed. Afraid of what she might say next.

But when nothing else came, I had to ask. "Do you? Have a thing for me?" I regretted it the moment I said it. The timing was off. Her mood was off. I looked down to my lap, as I could see Beck shake her head in my peripheral vision. I wished I had been more patient. The silence stretched between us, and though she was near, I felt our distance grow.

"You are so . . . infuriating! You waltz into my life after all these years, and I don't see where you fit in. I don't know where you belong in my life because I already have a best friend, and I already have a boyfriend. *Had* a boyfriend. Yet there's just something about you. About us. And I don't understand it. So, if you have to know if I have a thing for you . . ." Beck paused. She was talking herself out of what she really wanted. Her fear of being loved was swallowing her whole, and it was so loud, I could almost hear the turmoil between her ears.

"Beck, you deserve a life with no regrets. If I had to guess, you have a few from this weekend. Don't make another one. Tell me. Tell me how you really feel," I pleaded.

I could tell I struck a chord with her when tears filled her eyes. "I'd be lying if I told you there wasn't a piece of me that was drawn to you."

My heart pounded, and my hands balled into fists filled with the bed's comforter. Through clenched teeth, I asked what I knew I shouldn't: "How big is the piece, Beck?"

Her face was devoid of color. Whatever it was, I'd hit it on the head.

"I don't know," Beck whispered as tears streamed down her cheeks.

My lungs expanded, and I knew not to push further. I threw my head back and closed my eyes, basking in the small confession she had made. She didn't know how much yet, but she knew that some part of us belonged to one another. There was only one problem. Why did she look so afraid? I released my white-knuckled grip of the bedding and raked my hands through my hair. "OK, well we don't have to have it all figured out now. We can figure this out together." Concern filled the empty spaces in my mind until I could hardly think straight.

"I can't—"

My cell phone alarm chimed, loud and intrusive. I jumped to turn it off, but by the time I returned, the window of honesty had closed. The emotion that filled Beck's eyes was now dulled. Her walls were back up, and her feelings were hidden deep inside. I was left with more questions than answers. I should have felt like I had just won the lottery, but I felt no such victory.

"We can't be late for our flight." Beck threw off the blanket and bolted to the restroom, promptly shutting the door behind her. I let her be while I drowned in my fears. I gathered what little clothing I had and threw it into my suitcase. Then I picked up my laptop. It was when I opened my backpack to place it inside that I saw Beck's birthday gift. I stilled, not knowing if I should give it to her or not. I was almost positive the moment had passed. Several of them over the span of the weekend would have been preferable to this one. I set my laptop down and took the small bag out of my backpack. Reaching inside, I pulled out the small box that held the crystal dragonfly.

As soon as I saw the green wings, I felt the need to give it to her in this imperfect moment. *A piece of me* rang through my ears, swirling inside me—a song of hope. I clenched the tiny box to my chest and spun around with the determination to give it to Beck and the need for her to remember. It wasn't the perfect time, but the perfect time may never come for us. It had to be now. I knocked on the bathroom door.

"Yeah?" Beck asked.

"I have something for you." I placed my palm on the door jamb and leaned into it. Beck opened the door slowly. Her eyes found the tiny box for a moment before lifting to meet mine. "Here. It's your birthday gift."

"You didn't have to get me a—"

"I know. But I saw it, and it reminded me of you."

Beck opened the box. Nerves crawled under my skin like an army of ants, and I wanted to squirm. I crossed my arms over my chest and watched her intently. The green-bodied dragonfly emerged from the box and sparkled in Beck's hands. Her eyes, as green as the emerald wings, were transfixed on the gift. I couldn't tell how she felt about it. The seconds ticked on, and I felt more restless by her silence as the time passed.

What seemed like an eternity later, Beck lifted her gaze to meet mine, and I could see the recognition behind her puffy eyes.

Both of us jumped when a thunderous knock rapped against the hotel door, breaking the moment I had waited twenty-one years for.

"Time to go!" James yelled.

"Do you think Becca is in there with him?" Payton asked.

"Well she's not with Nolan," Brooklyn said.

Beck pushed past me, hand clasped around the dragonfly. She grabbed her suitcase and her bag, and I nearly jumped to get out of her path. She swung the door open. "Hi! You guys all ready?" Beck asked in a tone that I could only describe as the opposite. The opposite of everything she'd just conveyed with her eyes. The opposite of everything she felt when she held the crystal in her hand. Was this her plan? Were we just going to pretend this didn't happen?

I shoved my laptop into my backpack, a little more recklessly than I intended, and followed Beck out of the room with my suitcase in tow. James wagged his eyebrows at me and elbowed me in the ribs as the girls whispered a few feet down the hall. Nolan appeared in his doorjamb adjacent to mine, and the air shifted once again. For an instant, I thought he was going to say something. But it never came. The bags under his eyes said he'd had a sleepless night. James was good at diffusing and sucked Nolan into a story about a girl he met at the bar almost immediately. I dragged behind the group, lost in thought.

Beck kept her distance from both Nolan and me. She even worked hard at avoiding eye contact. I wished I could say the same for Payton and Brooklyn; they wouldn't stop staring. I wondered how much Beck was telling them. How much more they knew than I did. Beck knew she had feelings for me—that much was clear—but she didn't yet feel comfortable opening up to me. And if she couldn't talk to me, then it was possible that I would become the thing that she wanted but wouldn't allow herself to have. I'd essentially be the freefall she was too afraid of. Or the tattooed twig. I couldn't let that happen. I wouldn't be another failure in her life.

While waiting to board the plane, Brooklyn texted me from where she sat only one row away.

Do you want to sit with Beck on the flight home? I could sit with the guys.

It was a small act of kindness, but it meant the world to me.

You're the best!

When it was time to board the flight, Brooklyn positioned herself just behind James and Nolan. I trailed far behind the group, pretending to be consumed with e-mails on my phone. It wasn't *all* a lie. The real estate agent, Tina, had messaged me saying I was in escrow and there was an opportunity to rent before the purchase was complete. I'd be going home to my very own brown shag carpet. Brooklyn sat in the row with the guys, and when it was my turn to take a seat, the only one open was next to Payton, who was currently trying to get Brooklyn to sit in the open seat.

Brooklyn winked at me when I passed by, and I tried to hide my smile. James was still entertaining Nolan with nonstop chatter.

"Brooklyn, sit here!" Payton said. Heat crept over my face as I looked to Brooklyn. She placed a set of earbuds in, pretending not to hear. I pushed my suitcase overhead and Payton moved her purse out of my seat. By the time I had my backpack tucked under the seat before me and my seatbelt fastened, the row had turned ice cold. Beck stared out the window, and I wanted to reach out and take her hand. I would have if Payton wasn't in the middle of us.

It wasn't long after takeoff that Payton stuffed earbuds in her ears and closed her eyes. I tore off a piece of my napkin and chucked it at Beck. It hit the side of her head that drew a curtain between us. She patted the side of her head before pulling the balled-up napkin from her strands. She unraveled it, flipped it over, set it down, and looked back to the window. I did it again. She unfolded the napkin, then refused to look at me.

I found a pen in my backpack and took what was left of my napkin under my drink. Realizing I never told her how I felt, I knew I had to convey it somehow. But how do you tell the woman you love the depth of your feelings? How would I squeeze it onto half a napkin? I bit at the back of the pen, running it over my teeth.

When the idea came to me, I set pen to paper. I drew a small circle and labeled it "My piece." Then I drew the same thing again but labeled it "Your piece." Then I connected the two circles to make an infinity symbol. The drawing wasn't great, but it was still better than her tattoo, and she'd paid for that. I wadded up the napkin and chucked it square at her forehead. This time she looked at me with a frown. Was it wrong that I enjoyed her aggravation nearly as much as her laughter? But when she opened up the napkin and studied the drawing, her eyes took on a fresh look. And this one I liked the most.

CHAPTER 16

In need of a bed, I went to the hotel that night. I was tired from Sin City, and I wasn't yet ready to face the smell of my new home. Plus, I hadn't gotten the keys from Tina yet. All I wanted was a hot shower. Scorching hot. Then, a night's sleep that stripped me of my fears and breathed new hope into me. I wanted to wake with the morning sunlight and stretch my arms wide, thinking *I've got this!*

I showered in the searing water, which was enough to melt away my negative thinking and send it straight down the drain. Then, I sent Tina a brief e-mail about picking up the keys the next morning. I held my phone in my hand, wanting very much to text Beck but not knowing what to say. If only she had accidentally told everyone I was her boyfriend, this would be so much easier. But the truth was, she didn't need me this time. No, this time . . . I needed her.

I stared at my phone for some time before building the

courage to craft a text that wouldn't just be alluring but safe. More than friends, but friendly enough. It seemed near impossible until I deleted ninety-five percent of my text.

Meet me Monday in Clover. I have something I want to show you.

It wasn't a question, and I had given her no way out. I watched as the burbling bubbles told me she was already texting back, and my stomach knotted in anticipation. I wondered if she had been holding her phone in pursuit of texting me as well. I waited patiently at first, but when the bubbles disappeared and no text followed, I couldn't help but text her a time and address and hope for the best.

The address was that of my new house. Not that I wanted to put her off with the smell of mildew or the stains in the brown shag carpet, but more that I wanted her help. I wanted her input on what made a house a home. I wanted to take the focus off the tension between us, and fix something. Achieve *something*. It didn't have to be us right now, we had lives upon lives to figure us out. We just needed a small win, and maybe that came in the form of shopping for a rug or a sofa. Perhaps she would want to take on the challenge with me.

It was early Monday morning, and I packed my scant belongings from the hotel into my backpack. I grabbed a coffee in the hotel lobby—sure to put hair on a young boy's chest—before checking out. It was nice to finally close the door on the transient living that I'd done in my search for Beck. Now, it was time to put some roots down. I met with my realtor, Tina McFay, to sign the paperwork and pick up my keys. The escrow was just beginning, but I could rent for the first month, and the owner was kind enough to let me begin the renovations. Good thing too, because the house was inhabitable as it was.

I took the gold key in my hand and waved goodbye to Tina. It was a new beginning for me in a life that seemed to run on forever. Somehow, this house . . . this life . . . I could see with Beck. It was a new start for me. I cherished that. I stole another glance at my phone; it must have been the trillionth time. Beck still hadn't replied, and I had no idea if she would show today or not. I still had a couple of hours to kill before I would be stood up, and I had a long list of items I needed to purchase. The top of the list was a bed, but perhaps even above that was deodorizer and hand soap. The basics.

The smell of crisp pine trees rushed into my car as I opened my sunroof, and a concentrated ray of sunlight warmed my skin. It was a beautiful day for new beginnings. I hoped Beck would feel it too.

I may or may not have gone a little overboard at the hardware store. I hadn't realized it until I was faced with the problem of packing everything into the trunk of my car. Perhaps I should have waited on the bags of wood chips and the potted flowers. But the thought of live flowers in front of the house was one I was sure Beck would like. I couldn't pass on the gardening gloves covered in purple flowers, either. It was absolutely overboard. I was aware, but I did it anyway.

Amongst the entire gardening section that I had purchased and stuffed into my trunk, I also picked up a crowbar and sledgehammer. I was very much looking forward to using them both. There wasn't a particular wall or cabinet I was planning on removing right away, but I knew I wanted to hack something, and I thought I'd better be prepared.

By the end of the night, I would need to purchase a mattress and pillow so that I'd have a place to sleep. I didn't have time to do it now, in case Beck showed up, so I planned to make a run right before dinner time.

I pulled up to my new house just before noon. I would not call it a home for some time—not until it had earned the right. I turned my ignition off and stared at the old house hidden behind the growth of weeds and chipped brick. For a moment, I thought of the house as a metaphor for my life. Beaten down. Old beyond its days. And ready for new beginnings. A fire lit in my belly, and I wanted to transform the house immediately. Pour all of my tethered restraint and sorrows into it and make it something beautiful.

The car warmed in the absence of air conditioning, and I was forced to step out and meet my future, face to face. A lot of hard work lay before me, but I was grateful to have something to take my mind off of Beck. At least here, I could control the outcome.

I popped my trunk and sighed before starting my very long project. By the fourth bag of wood chips, I was ready to rip my shirt off and jump into the pool. There was no pool, of course. Not in this part of town. I pulled my shirt over my head and threw it into the trunk of my car before picking up the fifth and final bag of wood chips. Gravel crunched under the weight of tires behind me. I spun around with the bag on my shoulder to see a grey single cab truck pull into my driveway. I shielded the ray from my eyes and squinted into the light. I had hoped it was Beck, but I didn't recognize the truck. The windshield, lit up by a blaring glare of sunlight, hid the driver's identity.

"Is this your house?" Beck said as she stepped out of the truck. She came. A wash of relief fled through me.

"Is that your truck?" I answered with a question of my own.

Beck slid her phone into her back pocket and approached me at the trunk of my car. "It is." She played nervously with her keys. I watched her eyes drop, taking in my bare chest, and I felt somewhat exposed. I didn't bare the type of body she was accustomed to. I was no Nolan.

"Good! Because I'm going to need a truck!"

Beck nodded, knowing she was sucked in. "Is that why you called me here? Because you needed a truck?"

"No, I swear! I didn't even know you had one. But, uh . . . Now that I do, you absolutely have to help me. Like, a lot! I barely fit all of this into my car, and there's going to be more. A lot more," I said.

"Really?" Beck asked, peering into my car.

"Yeah. I don't even have a mattress to sleep on. I mean, what do you want me to do, sleep on the floor? Strap a mattress to the top of my car?" I twisted to the car behind me. Beck smiled. "It's the least you could do for a *friend,* right?"

"I suppose so." Beck rolled her eyes. "Do you need help bringing stuff in?"

"That would be great. Grab what you can. I'm going to toss this bag with the others," I said as I walked the bag I had slung over my shoulder to the pile I had made underneath the front window. I thought it would make a perfect place for a flower bed.

"Where do you want these?" Beck followed me with two pots of flowers in her arms.

"Here would be great!" I said. We continued to unpack my loot. The wood chips and flowers were finally unloaded, and what remained were bags that needed to be taken into the house. Beck made fun of me for the purple gardening gloves she spotted within the bag. I was too much of a coward to tell her I bought them for her. Instead, I claimed it was my favorite color. While it wasn't my favorite color, it was one that reminded me of a very revealing dress she once wore to her brother's wedding. And for that reason alone, it was a special color. We stacked as many bags as we could fit into our arms before heading inside, and I immediately regretted not attempting to air the house out before she came over.

"Remember how our parents were a part of that group when we were—oh my god! What is that smell!?" Beck hid her nose in the crook of her arm as the bags swung across her chest. It was worse than I'd remembered. The mildew.

"That's just mildew from the house being closed up for

so long. It should air out after we open some windows." We placed our bags on the nearby kitchen counter.

"That's *mildew*?" Beck asked with her face buried in her arm. For the first time since she got here, I was worried she wouldn't stay.

"Yeah, that's just—ack!" My stomach wrenched, vomit nearly propelling out of my mouth.

"Easton! That's *not* mildew!" Beck opened the backdoor slider and ran outside. I had no choice but to follow her.

"Yeah, that's just the smell. You'd be surprised. There's probably a wall with mold growing rampantly underneath the drywall or something. But, um, don't worry. I bought a candle," I said looking back at the bags on the kitchen counter. They seemed so close yet so far away.

"*A candle*?" Beck looked at me with eyes of doubt.

"Yeah, I mean, it's a mosquito candle"—my voice rose—"but they put off a smell, and I figured it was better than nothing. I'm just going to open all the windows and doors and light that candle. We'll be inside in no time!" I really wished I had my shirt to hide my nose in, but I had to use my hand instead. I ran through the house, opening the windows and doors while breathing through my mouth. My tongue pressed firmly against my teeth. When I crossed the threshold of the kitchen into the hall, I realized the smell was originating somewhere around the stove. I ran to the backyard and gasped, more dramatically than intended. Beck laughed at me. I stood shirtless and sweaty in front of her, my hands on my hips.

"Have you had lunch yet?" I asked.

"I could eat. I could always eat."

I smiled, thinking back to a time when Beck was sick and her appetite fleeting. It was nice to hear she'd gotten it back.

"Change of plans. Let's let this whole thing breathe," I circled my hand toward the house, "while we get lunch. And a mattress." I looked down to the ground, hoping she wouldn't protest. I couldn't be more relieved when she agreed to spend the day with me.

"There's only one problem," Beck said.

"What's that?" I asked.

Beck pointed through the slider to the front door, "We've got to get to the other side."

I laughed, and a split second later I had her hand in mine as we ran through the house in one breath. Beck was laughing on the other side, and I was left wondering how such a rancid stench—which was definitely *not* mildew— could have possibly brought a smile to her face. I took my shirt from the trunk of my car and pulled it on as I jumped into the passenger's side of Beck's truck.

"Are you just going to leave your doors open like that?" Beck started her ignition.

"Are you kidding me? There's nothing to steal, and if there were, I don't think the burglar would survive in there!"

"Good point!" Beck said as she backed out of my driveway.

It was when Beck asked for directions to the store that I found my opportunity to cross the New River Bridge with her by my side. There were two ways out of town, and I led her to the one that crossed the bridge. The closer the bridge drew, the more I feared her reaction. It felt almost cruel. Like I had been hiding this secret of who she was and then forcing her to remember. I thought I had done the right thing by letting her memory come back to her slowly, but now I worried I should have spilled the truth long ago. Like any friend would. I immediately felt the weight of my decision as the bridge drew closer.

CHAPTER 17

My heart thumped in my chest as I wiped my clammy palms on my pant legs. The New River Bridge was right around the corner, and we would cross it soon. Beck messed with her phone as she tried to pay attention to the road and find the perfect song at the same time. I was worried that she would miss it altogether . . . but even more worried she wouldn't. It was possible that she had been on her phone when she crossed it the first time on her way to my house, had she taken the bridge.

"Did you come to my house this way or did you take the backside of the mountain?" I asked.

Beck set her phone in her lap and surveyed her surroundings. "Um?" She looked out her window, eyebrows scrunched.

The truck jolted when it lifted onto the steel bridge. My eyes rested heavily on Beck's. She placed her foot on the brake and the truck crawled to a stop. What was she doing?

I looked out my window. A teen girl was stuck on the side of the bridge with a flat tire. We had just gotten onto the bridge, and I didn't want to stop here, but Beck found it in her heart to stop and ask the girl if she was alright. Beck rolled down my window and yelled, "Do you need help?"

The girl examined us before saying, "Not unless you know how to change a tire?"

Beck looked at me, and I nodded with a sigh. "Yeah, I'll just pull over!"

As I stood on the side of the bridge, jacking the car up, I realized it was the exact lie I fabricated when Beck's father asked how we met. Beck, however, was the girl with the flat tire in the version I had told. As I listened to the girls chat, I suddenly became worried that Beck's dad would pass us on the bridge and see his daughter standing on the side of the road with her deceased boyfriend. It wasn't a good look for either of us, and I had been foolish enough to forget my baseball hat in my car.

I lifted the replacement tire out of the girl's trunk and slid it onto the post. I listened for hesitation in Beck's voice, but I detected no signs of despondency. I worked as quickly as I could to move the girl off the bridge without Beck and I becoming discovered. Relief washed over me when the girl drove away in her lopsided car, which now had three regular tires and one miniature one. Only two cars had passed by in that time, and from what I could tell, they were no one of importance in Beck's past life.

"Thanks for doing that. I just remember what it was like being a new driver, and I'm glad that we could help her." Beck started back for her truck.

"Oh hey! Look at that, want to take a quick look?" I pointed down the bridge and hated myself for it. But the truth was, if Beck didn't figure it out soon, I might just blurt it out over lunch.

Beck hesitated, "Um, we should really get you that mattress."

"Come on. Just real quick. I bet it's . . . something to be remembered." I cringed. I was the worst.

With Beck's truck already pulled off to the side of the road, we walked a quarter of the way down the bridge. Beck was quiet—even more so than usual—and I could tell she was teetering on the cusp of uncomfortable and full-blown panic. I watched with large eyes.

"Do you feel alright?" I asked, stopping when I reached the spot in which we met.

Beck's face was devoid of color. "I'm OK. I'm just scared of heights."

"You seemed OK when we were on the skyscraper . . . apart from the jumping that is," I said.

"Yeah, that was different." Beck looked over the edge with a deeply creased forehead. I peered over the edge with her. It was a long way down, and the water was moving more freely than the night we had met. Beck pulled at the neck of her shirt. "Do. Do you ever get that feeling," she whispered, barely audible, "that you've been here before?"

My stomach dipped over and over. "What do you mean?" I asked.

"I feel like I've been here before. Like, physically, *right here.*" Beck ran her hands along the top of the railing. Her eyes ticked back and forth, looking for answers. She paused before peeking at me, "I feel like I've been right here . . . with *you*."

I sucked in a deep breath, wishing I had a plan. A map. Any protocol to follow. But this was a new situation, and I didn't get many of them anymore. I'd figured all of this out on my own over the course of my first couple of lives. Nobody was there to hold my hand through it, and I didn't know if I was pushing her too fast. Or perhaps it was too slow?

"Oh my god, don't listen to me. I'm crazy. I'm a crazy person!" Beck nodded her head to herself as if she had repeated that mantra her whole life. I hurt for her.

"You're *not* crazy," I rebutted.

"Yes, I am. You have no idea. You think you know me, but you don't."

It pained me to see her struggle. I knew what she was going through, and I knew I had all but one of the answers she sought. All but why. I didn't know why it happened to me, to her, or to any other Tethered Soul.

"If you're crazy, Beck, then I'm crazy too."

She raised her eyebrows as if I was making light of the situation. Like I couldn't possibly understand what she was talking about.

"What, you're crazy *about* me, I take it?" Beck rolled her eyes dismissively, and I could sense her panic dissipating.

"I'm a lunatic for you! I just can't get enough of you! And I *do* know you. I understand how you feel, right now," I said. The corners of her lips lifted.

"I feel like I've known you my entire life. Is that weird?" she asked.

I pushed off the bridge and pulled her into my arms. She felt like home. "You have," I said, and I didn't mean since we were kids. There was nothing like holding Beck in my arms. It was like allowing two magnets to click together. The birds crowed above, and the warmth of the sun hit my back. "You're probably getting hungry. Do you want to go get that lunch now?" I asked.

"Yeah, let's do that," Beck said with a kind smile. I slid my hand down her arm and interlocked my hand in hers. But as I started for her truck, Beck's hand slipped from mine. She stopped clear in her tracks and her face fell flat and cold. It was the moment I feared most.

I did a double-take, my hand feeling more than a void in her absence. "Beck, what's—"

"What is that?"

I turned to follow Beck's trembling, accusatory finger. My throat dried and my insides melted. Beck pointed to our memorial plaque. I raked my hands through my hair as she slowly squatted, examining it. Her head tilted ever so slightly as I waited for destiny to rear its ugly head. And I knew *I* had brought this on myself. On her. Beck swiped her fingers over the plaque and abruptly stood, tears filling her eyes. "Never mind! Let's go."

"Beck, wait!" I called out to her, but she kept walking. Unfortunately for her, fate was not something she could run from. I picked up my pace and grabbed her by the shoulder. "Beck, I think we need to talk." I placed my emphasis on *think*, because again, I did not know what was best for her. It was a lose-lose situation, and at this point, my only real hope was that I wouldn't lose Beck all together.

"What! About what? What could you possibly know about what I'm going through? Unless you *do*. Unless you *have*. Unless you've *kept it* from *me*!" Beck stretched her arms out wide, baring her open heart as an easy target.

"What if I told you, that . . . when I walk out on this bridge, I get memories, too?"

Beck's arms slowly dropped to her side and her eyes slanted in pain. Her face was soaked with sympathy and stained with fury.

"What if I told you that . . . I know why you're afraid of the water?" A small sound came burbling from Beck's throat, and she cupped both her hands over her mouth. "What if I told you, that you are my . . . home? And that I've loved you since *before* you moved in next door." I shrugged.

I didn't know what else to tell her, but it sure as hell would not be that we were already married! Not yet anyway—not while she was a flight risk. *Home.* The word stuck in my head. It wasn't the perfect choice, yet it was the closest thing to it. And somehow, it held more meaning than love. The word used by every other person in this world with a crush or infatuation. But none of them had survived death for their loved one. We had something unique, and it didn't have a title.

Beck swiped a tear that fell from her eye, and she peered back at the bridge behind me. She pointed down at the large arch but couldn't choke out what she wanted to.

"You remember, don't you? Some of it, at least?" I asked. Beck's head shook up and down. Demanding. "I can fill in the blanks, Beck. If you let me," I pled. Closing the distance between us, I placed my hand on her shoulder, but she shrugged away. She'd turned to stone. Sharp as an arrow. And I was her target.

"I only have one question. Who. Are. *Those people?*" Beck's pointer finger shot out like a cannon and exploded into a plume of accusation and betrayal.

I looked down the bridge, fearful of who I might see, then grabbed my chest and sighed when nobody was there except the gentle spring breeze. "Which people?"

"*Those* people, Easton! The ones that had this entire bridge dedicated to them! Who are they!? Because one of them is *you* . . . and I don't know the other!" Beck yelled, her voice splintering into past and present lives.

I was so worried for Beck, I'd forgotten all about my name being on the plaque. I rubbed my eyes, shaking my head at the impossible situation that I'd found myself in. "OK, you want to know the truth?" My voice had risen to match hers. It wasn't the time to lose myself, but I was exploding with repressed emotions, and her tone was taunting me. "Those people, Beck! Those people who died on this bridge twenty-one years ago . . . *They're us!*" I threw my hand down, driving my point home. *Home.* I watched as Beck became unglued. Large tears streamed down her face, and her pale complexion was now red in the heat of the battle.

My heart pounded in my chest, and I could hear the blood pumping between my ears. I regretted yelling at her and needed to show her how sorry I was. That I'd be there for her. I reached out for her as she stepped back. Her body was trembling.

"No! Don't touch me!" Beck's eyes laced with the fear of the unknown. "*You.* You're the crazy one!" Beck took one more slow step back.

"Beck, don't do this," I pled.

"*You're crazy!*" Beck screeched, fleeing to her truck. She started her ignition as I tried to open the passenger's side door, but by the time the door was half open she'd hit the gas and sped off, nearly taking my arm with her. I stumbled, trying to catch my footing as I jogged into the middle of the bridge with my arms reached out wide.

"Beck! Come on! *Fuck!*" I spun on my heels as a car horn sounded too close for comfort. And this time . . . this time, it *was* Beck's dad.

I leaped out of the way, and for a split second, he and I locked eyes. "Damn it!" I said to myself, tilting my head up to the blue sky, my hands square on my hips.

I took to the edge of the New River Bridge, thinking of the day I almost jumped. My heart had filled with sorrow as the rain pelted down on me. I'd lost everyone I'd ever loved. And worse, I had stopped letting them in. I had locked my heart up so tight, I couldn't breathe. I'd been mourning for hundreds of years but somehow still found a way to hurt myself worse. I'd been suffocating, and as I stood on the bridge's rail, I knew that it could all be gone in a moment's time. My pain erased. And for a few short years, I would forget all the agony I'd brought onto myself. And in that moment, I had committed to starting over.

That was, until Beck had pulled over. Her green eyes had shone even in the storm's wrath, her life burning bright as the end neared. I took pity on her at first, but quickly felt my heart beating again. I hadn't felt that alive in centuries, and I had no idea what it was. Not until she tried to distance herself from me had I realized that my heart was opening to her. And as I'd taken her in, all the pain from lives lost simply fell into place. Like the ebb and flow of an ocean's current—lives lived, lives lost, lives journeyed onward. And somehow, Beck's love had showed me how to accept it all. She'd thought she needed me because she was dying. But really, I needed her, because I was living and I didn't know how.

CHAPTER 18

Stranded with nothing more than my toxic stream of conscious worry, I walked toward the new house. At some point, I'd call for a taxi, but for now, it was probably best for me to walk off some steam. It wasn't the first time Beck and I had fought, but it was the first time she'd found out her life was a lie. All of it. Every single thing she knew to be true, shattered in a moment's time. I didn't try to convince myself that I understood. Instead, I took out my phone and texted her to come back. I begged her to turn around and talk to me. Five text messages later, and she hadn't replied. Not even burbling dots, a sign of an attempt. Three phone calls later and she had turned off her phone altogether.

I walked a couple of miles before calling for a ride, but it still wasn't enough to clear my mind. And I imagined no amount of miles would cure what had manifested in my heart, soul, and gut. As if the day couldn't get any worse, the taxi dropped me off at the house that had been left to air out. I hadn't even gotten my mattress.

Later that night, I was fortunate enough to find a dead raccoon tucked behind my refrigerator. It was a monstrous pile of fur decomposing in the tight space. Tiny worms slurped through the open holes in its flesh. The sight was enough to make someone sick, and I had a long debate in my head over which was worse: the sight or smell. After the debate was settled—it was the smell—I used all of my trash bags as gloves. The better option was the purple gardening gloves, but I still wanted to keep those for Beck, in case she returned. *When* she returned. I scooped up the rotting raccoon and ran him to the nearest outside trashcan. As for the juices left behind, I'd have to wait until I bought bleach and rags from the store the following day.

I skipped dinner. I'd like to say it was because of a broken heart, but truthfully, it was a combination of the hollow feeling inside my heart *and* the worms that took my appetite away. I'd nearly thrown up three times when taking the body out. It wasn't a strength of mine. No matter how many awful things I'd seen in my time, my stomach never grew stronger. Nor did my gag reflex, which matched that of a teenage girl. The smell had improved greatly with the removal of the raccoon, and I left the windows open to vent the house that night. When the sky grew dark and the air chilly, I retreated to my car. It would be a miserable night without sleep, but I couldn't bring myself to crawl back to the hotel when I had just bought a house. Maybe it was the stubborn part of me, but I'd sleep in my car for a week if I had to. It wouldn't be the first time, and I was sure it wouldn't be the last.

Bundled in two jackets, I used a pair of rolled-up jeans as a pillow. At some point in the night, I fell asleep despite the cold and discomfort. I woke frequently to unknown noises and nightmares centered upon the New River Bridge. It was Beck and I drowning again in a trapped car and her eyes watching me painfully. It was my death in 1727 when I was trapped in a burning house. Smoke filled my lungs as the heat encapsulated me. It was World War I when a bullet pierced my chest. Blood drained slowly until my limbs ran cold and I no longer feared what lay ahead. It was my first life . . . when I died as a child at the hands of my father. Beck watched them all while I lived every death, back-to-back. I'd never felt so exposed—not in my unconscious or waking hours. I had a lot of history to unpack, and the look in her eyes reminded me that I was not normal. Nor would I ever come to be.

I tried to sleep after waking in a puddle of my own sweat, but after the nightmare, I lay across my back seat, forcing shut my eyelids and racing mind. Losing Beck would be worse than all my deaths put together. Would she still want me now that the truth had been exposed? I didn't know how much of it was within my control, but if she had become a Tethered Soul because of her bond to me, I'd have to believe that she wouldn't walk away. At least, not in *every* lifetime.

Since I couldn't fall back to sleep, I was up before sunrise. It was one of the most beautiful views our earth offered, yet so many rarely saw it because it was easier to stay nestled in the warmth of blankets. Today, not only did I want to see the sunrise, but I needed it. Watching the morning unfold, my existence was a fresh slate, which made the necessity to move forward with Beck all the clearer. And if I was being honest, my house could use a couple of extra hours airing out.

I started my car and cranked on the heat before making my way to a nearby gas station. It was there that I got not one but two coffees. The gas station clerk sympathized with me and the dark gaunt rings framing my eyes. She told me I should go back to bed, and whatever I had planned for the day could wait a few extra hours. I smiled warmly, but I knew that there was no hiding from my problems—the same way that Beck couldn't hide from hers. They'd be there, life after life, always waiting. And while the extra sleep would sure be nice to rid the fire from my eyes, it wouldn't make my day any easier.

I double-fisted my coffees to the car and started up the mountain. There were many spots with spectacular views and places large enough to park a couple of cars side by side. I pulled into the very first one I came upon as the sky lightened. I checked my phone again, but there were no messages from Beck.

I wondered if I should go to the college and continue my charades of being a student or if I should give her the space and truth that she deserved. Personally, I wanted to track her down, spew the truth out all over her and give her no other choice but to absorb it. If she was going to leave me, it better be that she knew the truth and still chose a different path. I wasn't OK, however, with her leaving me under any misconceptions of who I was or what had happened. Still, I knew what I *should* do. Respect her space. Give her time to compartmentalize. Allow her to come back to me all on her own.

The sun released its brightly burning rays from the horizon and I watched with a sorrow-filled heart. They say it's better to have loved and lost than never to have loved at all. And as I watched the full strength and beauty of the sun emerge that morning, I agreed. Heartbreak was worth it. Sure, my life would go on in endless despair for centuries to come, but I was better for knowing her.

I wasn't surprised to see an unknown vehicle sitting in my driveway when I pulled up to my house, even though I had invited no one. Before I could park my car, I saw Brooklyn, with her long, dark-chocolate locks, emerge from the vehicle. She slammed her door and crossed her arms at her chest. I didn't know what was coming, but I could make an educated guess.

"Good morning, Brooklyn. I see you found my house," I said.

"Easton, I don't know what the hell you have done to Becca, but you've really thrown a wrench in my plan," Brooklyn snapped.

"Your plan?"

"I basically had her feeding out of your hand! And this is how you repay me? Could you have . . . less game?"

I'd never seen this side of sweet Brooklyn, but I never doubted it existed. "What are you talking about?" I grabbed my bag of bleach and rags from my trunk and walked up to my house. Brooklyn was quick on my heels.

"You said she was your soulmate! I've been doing everything in my power to match you two up. And then you unravel it in one afternoon! She never wants to see you again, and what's worse than that? She went running to Nolan last night!" Brooklyn shut the door behind us and her nose wrinkled when the air hit her nostrils.

"Nolan!"

"Yes!"

"Well, why did you let that happen?" I said.

"Me?" Brooklyn's jaw dropped.

"I'm sorry. You're right, I know. I'm sorry," I said. Placing the bag on the counter, I mindlessly pulled out my cleaning supplies while I told myself I deserved this. A long stint of silence spanned between us. "I'm sorry, why are you here?" I asked, suddenly confused.

"You sure do have a lot to learn, you know that?" Brooklyn scowled.

I threw the rags down on top of the plastic grocery bag and gave her my full attention. Whatever she came here to say, she'd better say it before I shut the door on her. I was in no mood, and she didn't know what she was talking about.

"And I suppose you've got it all figured out?" I asked.

"Well, a lot more than you have. I mean, what have you been doing all of this time, anyway?"

I looked around the house and turned up my palms. "I bought a house. And I took a decomposing dinosaur to the trash last night with my bare hands. I bought a bed. What have you been doing?" My brows knitted together. My fondness for Brooklyn was fading.

"Oh my god." Brooklyn's face displayed a mixture of confusion and amusement, but mostly it was the amusement that twinkled in her warm honey eyes. "You don't know?" she asked, though it was more of a statement.

I looked her up and down, from head to toe and back again. What was she hiding from me? I let out a slow, measured breath and then asked. "Know what?" in a tone that was sharper than I intended.

Two car doors slammed shut, and I knew that my bed had arrived at the worst possible time. "Know what, Brooklyn?"

Her eyes flicked to the front door as a loud knock rapped against it. For a second, I stilled, giving her the opportunity to explain, but when she didn't speak up, I went to open the door.

"Hello. I have a setup today for Easton Green."

"Yes, that's me."

"Sign right here." I signed the paperwork against the door and handed it back to the man wearing blue coveralls. "If you show us where you would like it set up, we can get started."

"Absolutely. Right this way."

The men came in, carrying several large boxes. I shot a look to Brooklyn, begging her to wait, but when I returned, she was already gone.

It was nearly three days before Beck showed up at my front door. And when I realized she'd come back to me, I had the distinct feeling that Brooklyn was partially to thank. Beck stood with a bag of hot food and a can of deodorizer spray in hand. We stared at each other, sizing one another up in silence. So much tension passed between us, but I still wasn't sure where she stood. From what I could tell, she was here to say her goodbyes, and for that, I wasn't ready. "You're early. I wasn't expecting you for a week, or two."

Beck rolled her eyes. "You weren't at school . . ."

It was as good of a time as any to flush out my lies. "I don't attend Norton University, so there was no point in going to school if you didn't want to talk to me."

Beck's eyes lifted as she took it in. I could see her wheels turning. She was questioning other things I had told her. I ran my hand over my jaw and looked down at her shoes. Her feet twisted in trepidation.

"Look, I'm sorry I left you on the side of the road. It was kind of an asshole move."

"It was," I agreed.

"I feel like . . . I should run wildly in the opposite direction from you. But what can I say? You have this weird piece of me. You always have."

"We belong together, Beck. Don't run from me. *Stay*." I encouraged her.

"Well, I wouldn't have come with dinner for two if I was going to apologize and leave. Can I come in?" she asked.

"Oh, yeah, come in." I held the door open and resisted running my hand down her back as she passed by me.

"It's . . . surprisingly better." Beck shrugged. "But I think I should still spray this." She gave her can a little shake.

"Yeah, go ahead."

Beck walked around the house spraying an obscene amount of deodorizer into the air while I sorted out the bag of food she had brought over. I didn't have the heart to tell her I'd already eaten. "I can't believe mildew smells that bad!" Beck muttered.

"I think I've gotten used to it. I barely smell it anymore. But let's take the food outside," I said. There was a small stone bench in the backyard we could eat our dinner on. Beck nearly emptied the can in the kitchen air before joining me outside.

"I'm actually a little surprised you came back. I mean, I knew you would at some point, but I wasn't entirely sure how long you would make me wait," I said.

"I didn't want to come back here," Beck said.

My jaw tightened, and my stomach dipped, "You didn't?"

"As you could probably imagine, I have a lot of negative emotions associated with you. It's no cakewalk to look at your face and wonder if something was real or a nightmare." Beck's hair fell in front of her face, and she tucked it behind her ear.

I nodded, hating the way my very face brought her pain. "Then why are you here?"

"I have . . . so many questions. I have questions so loud I can see them when I close my eyes. I have so many questions that I'm physically sick. My stomach is knotted, and my is head pounding. And if I have to go through one more night like I had for the last few nights, I might as well drown myself all over again!" My gut wrenched. Beck swallowed hard and looked down at her lap as she placed one soft hand over her mouth. Then, timidly, she turned to me. "That is what happened, right? We drowned?"

I re-wrapped my taco and placed it back in the bag. There was no way I could eat my way through this conversation. "What exactly do you remember?" It was as good as any place to start.

Beck's knees bounced, and she looked up to the dusky sky. "Honestly, I remember nothing. I have these flashes, though. They're like, um . . . like snapshots of memory. I've always thought they were repetitive dreams, and I'd had them so many times that they burned into my mind like a genuine memory would. I have this . . . memory? I guess you would call it? Um, it's of us, and we're underwater. There's blood all around, and it's cold yet numb at the same time. And I can just close my eyes, and you're still there, still staring at me with those glacier blue eyes, until . . . until you're not anymore."

Beck's eyes shifted, and her voice fragmented. She lifted her hand and shrugged her shoulders in doubt. "I don't know? I don't know. This is all so stupid! I don't know what to believe!"

I pulled her in for a hug and this time she allowed me to comfort her. She buried her head into my chest, and I wrapped my arms around her back.

"And I feel things too! Like I have some sort of weird

gravitational pull to you, and I knew there had to be an answer, but I just couldn't figure it out! I want to feed the homeless! Like, I think about it *all* the time!" Beck choked out in a half cry, half laugh into my shoulder.

My face contorted in amusement and torture. Neither of us was able to define the flood of emotions tied to something so unlikely. I wanted her pain to stop first and foremost, but then I wanted to tell her stories of our past life. I wanted to see her laughing again. And I dreamed of fast-forwarding to the part where we left off twenty-one years ago. "I know it's hard. I've gone through it too."

"You have?" Beck pulled away, suddenly optimistic.

"Yeah, a long, long time ago."

Her eyes narrowed as she tried to stifle her cry. "What does that mean?" She frowned with a subtle warning that I must answer her question but in a way that wouldn't add to her already overloaded consciousness.

"I have this . . . *gift*?" I questioned myself by her reaction, and when she didn't completely lose it, I continued attentively. "When my life ends, I simply get the opportunity to do it all over again." Beck's reservation was painted in the creases of her forehead. "And now, you have this gift too!" I couldn't look her in the eye when I said it. I had always viewed my gift as a curse. A cage binding me to this world. I would never meet my maker or see what was on the other side of the veil.

CHAPTER 19

ow, you're immortal? *I'm* immortal!?" She'd been sucked into my phony optimism. I'd sold it for more than it was worth.

"Well, no. Not technically."

"Oh . . ."

"Immortal people don't die. We're the opposite. We die . . . a lot." And when it passed my lips, I knew I could no longer sell this as a gift.

I watched carefully as Beck started to see the controversy, but I desperately wanted her to think that this was a legacy we were chosen for. And perhaps we were? "But we get to do it together! And after a couple of times, you will have a pretty good memory of it all. It's only the beginning when your subconscious blocks out these memories of past lives. It's a defense mechanism, really."

Beck fiddled with the taco wrapper between her fingers. "You remember all of your past lives?" Beck looked at me with pink puffy eyes and a hint of hope. She was taking this better than I'd thought.

"Yes, I remember all of my lives. My last one is where I met you. And we fell so deeply in love, somehow, you became Tethered as well."

"Tethered?" Beck asked.

"Yeah, there's a name for our condition. *Gift.* We're called Tethered Souls, or at least that seems to be the most common name I've heard amongst our kind. I guess it makes sense because our soul is bound to keep coming back. But since I met you, I've questioned that."

"What do you mean?"

"Um, I just mean that I've never known a Tethered Soul to love another, and I question its meaning." I shrugged, and Beck stared at me like I was an open book she could no longer process. All the answers were there before her, ready for her to pick up, but she couldn't.

"There are others?" Beck said in a worried tone.

I waved my hand. "Don't even worry about that. They're just people," I said. She fed off of my temperament, and I could sense that her anxiety had started to dissipate. Her flustered skin was finally regaining its usual pale tone, and her breathing had slowed to a steady ebb and flow. We sat in silence until our attention fell to our dinner. Beck took her food out of the bag, and we ate in my backyard in reflection.

"Thanks for dinner," I said, breaking the silence. Beck was so emotionally drained that she could barely respond. Her eyes glassed over as she chewed slowly and methodically. "Hey! I have the best idea!" Beck's dreary face turned ever so slightly in my direction, as if she'd just woken from a deep sleep. Her flaxen hair draped over the corners of her eyes. "Do you want to demolish something?"

Beck brushed her hair from her face and tucked it behind her ear. "Like what?"

"Literally, anything!" The edge of her lips curled upwards as the light returned to her eyes, one sparkle at a time. "I bought this sledgehammer, and we can just . . ." I shook my thumb back at the house with an impish smile.

"Really?" Beck asked.

"I've always wanted an open floor plan!" I said with a shrug.

Beck picked up the sledgehammer with a gleam in her eyes. She found her grip while she lifted it up and down, trying to get a feel for the heaviness. I pointed to the wall that separated the dining room from the living room, and she approached it with determination. She took a wide stance as if she were playing baseball and took one last approving look in my direction with brows raised.

"Wreck it!" I hollered through cupped hands. Beck took a deep breath and swung the sledgehammer into the wall, yelping as it struck the drywall. She flinched, and the hammer stuck in the middle of the wall. Beck shook her hands and wiped them on her jeans. From my particular angle, I could see the hammer poking out on the other side of the wall.

"I . . . I need to try again. That one was just practice!"

Beck tried to pull the hammer out of the wall, but when it didn't budge, she stopped and looked toward me for help.

"You can do it!" I said.

Beck tried some more before turning her frustration onto me. "Seriously, the thing is stuck!" She slapped her palm on her side.

"Use your foot for leverage!" I said, busying myself as I tried to set up my Bluetooth speaker. Just finding the settings app was difficult enough amongst the sea of unused apps on my phone. Pairing was going to take me a while.

"Eerrr" Beck growled, and I turned, amused, just in time to see the sledgehammer break free and Beck propel backward onto her butt. The sledgehammer went flying backward over her head, clamoring down to the floor.

"Beck! Are you OK?" I approached her with an open hand for help up, but she wasn't ready. Her chest was rising and falling in pure frustration. Her face was beet red, and loose strands of her hair lifted with each huff. As soon as I smiled, I knew it was the wrong reaction. Her brows furrowed, and her eyes squinted into a devilish glare. It was precisely the reason why my smile grew to an outburst of laughter. Beck liked that even less. She scrambled to her feet and grabbed the hammer that landed several feet behind her. "Wow, take it easy!" I said, baring my palms.

She didn't. Every bit of frustration, anger, and fear came barreling out on that wall, and this time when she struck it, she didn't recoil. The music kicked on, stoking Beck's internal fire, and she tore into the wall as if it were every lie ever fed to her, every misconception she ever had, and every mistrusted person in her life. She broke into that wall like it was her cancer, and she'd had enough.

I wasn't going to admire the view from afar, although it was quite satisfying. I wanted in on the action. To destroy that demon with her. Together. I picked up my crowbar and hooked it into a hole she had torn into the wall. Then ripped the side of the drywall off. It was too easy. I tossed the crowbar over my shoulder as Beck took another overhead hack into the wall. I kicked at the exposed beam and it cracked. The music blared, and the beat drove another kick. The beam snapped in half.

Beck's face was flushed, and pieces of her hair stuck to the sweat on her forehead. She took a moment to catch her breath before she tossed the sledgehammer onto the ground and tried her hand at kicking the beams with me. She wasn't quite strong enough to get it on her first or second try, but the house was old and the beams gave way after a handful of her tries.

"This is for living a lie!" She kicked the beam and then looked toward me, waiting.

"This is for . . . having to lie!" I broke another beam in half.

Beck scowled at me, not quite approving of my confession. Then she let it go and yelled over the music, "This is for Nolan, that cheating son of a bitch!" She slammed a right hook into the only clean patch of drywall.

"Ahhh!" Beck pulled her hand back and tucked it in between her thighs, doubled over, holding her breath. The music blared on in the absence of our demolition.

I placed my hand on her back and waited for her to

stand upright again. When I was convinced that would never happen, I lowered to my knees and gently pulled her hand out from between her legs. Without the pressure against her hand, blood rose to the surface of her knuckles. "Wow, you really did it, didn't you?" I looked up to see Beck's teary eyes and full cheeks.

"He deserved it!" Beck said as she lifted her hand to examine the damage.

I huffed and pointed to her bloodied hand. "But did your hand deserve that?" I asked. Beck rolled her eyes and pushed her shoulder into mine, causing me to take a step back to catch my balance. I smiled at her, then looked back to the wall. If I hadn't known better, I'd say a bomb went through the center of it. "It's just what I wanted," I said as I framed the wall between my hands. Beck laughed, and I went to the kitchen to turn off the music and fetch her some ice from the freezer. Making do with what I had, I wrapped the ice in a small hand towel and took it to her. She held her hand out, trembling as I took it in mine and slowly lowered the ice down onto her knuckles. Beck winced, and I lifted the ice off for a moment before placing its full weight on top of her hand. "How's that?" I asked.

Beck nodded, still panting from the workout. Heat radiated off her body, and I found a subtle comfort in the way her chest rose and fell with every breath. Pressed against my own, her palm was moist and hot. The whole thing made my heart regain its momentum, though I had been still for some time. I examined the green flecks in Beck's eyes before my gaze dropped to her mouth as she bit down into her bottom lip. She was so close I could smell her cherry lip balm. But it wasn't enough. I needed to taste it, too.

I lowered my lips to hers, and my chest exploded when she lifted onto her toes to meet me in the middle. My eyes closed, allowing me to see more clearly than I had in months. It was the moment that I was sure I could live this life over and over, and every drop of insanity would all be worth it. Beck backed me up against a standing beam in the ruined wall. My back pressed into shards of broken drywall as I deepened my kiss. She responded with matched passion and urgency. The flutter in my chest swelled. The heat in my belly deepened lower yet.

I carefully took my hand off the ice and ran my hands up into Beck's hair. The ice pack slapped against the floor, and ice cubes kicked back at my legs. Beck wrapped one icy hand under my jaw while the hot one slid under my shirt and up my back. All the tension I'd carried with me came to a head in this heated moment, and I swept her up into my arms and carried her to my bedroom. She planted kisses down the side of my neck as I hurried down the hall. Grateful that I'd bought a bed just days earlier.

I took a deep breath, allowing my lungs to be filled to maximum capacity. Then, ever so slowly, I let all the strain I'd been living expel in one exhalation. The boulder had spared me, and I was unscathed.

Sometime after the passion had settled, when all was right in the world, and when Beck had finally found her way back into my arms, I closed my eyes and basked in the sublime. I could finally breathe again. We stayed there entangled as the sky grew black, and the house darkened.

When Beck pulled away, I tucked my hands behind my head and watched her pull her shirt over her head and shimmy into her jeans. Her eyes trailed around the empty bedroom before settling on the bare mattress and sleeping bag tangled underneath me. "Is this all you have?" she asked.

"Yeah. For tonight."

Beck singled out a thick lock of hair and wrapped it around her mouth, hiding her smile. A chuckle escaped me, though I was unsure why. She'd just looked so cute. So happy.

"You need me," Beck said, sitting next to me.

I smiled and placed my hand on her knee. There was absolute truth to what she said. It was even an understatement. The moonlight cast shadows across the side of her face, and even then, her beauty was undeniable. "I love you, Beck," I said as sure as the day we wed.

A slight curvature spread across her lips before she turned her head away and ran a hand through her hair. I wasn't expecting to hear it back, nor did I need to. But I did have to tell her how I felt.

"I—" Beck started.

"You don't have to say it back. I understand," I said, sitting up to rub her back.

"No, I want to, it's just—" Beck's shoulders rose.

"Shhh." I hushed her, leaning forward to kiss her on the forehead.

"I struggle because I feel like I know you," Beck went on, pointing her good hand at her heart and tapping her chest. "But here . . ." She pushed a finger to the side of her temple. "I don't have the pieces."

Though I understood, it was difficult to be told that you were forgettable. Especially after the love we had just made.

"I just need a little more time."

I forced a smile, thankful that my face was hidden in the shadows. "Well, you're in luck, because there's an unlimited number of days for you and me. Take all the time you need, but no more, you hear?" I said.

"OK, deal," Beck said with a smile.

Beck and I spent another hour sitting on my bare mattress, discussing her past relationships. Nolan included. She had anticipated that he wouldn't be faithful, but it never kept her from trying with him. Her intentions were to have fun, but she wound up liking him more than she planned. Because of that, she was hurt when he did what she knew he would. She talked about how she had an unhealthy pattern of picking guys who either couldn't commit or couldn't keep her attention. Of course, she didn't need to tell me. I already knew from the conversations we shared before. Still, I enjoyed her new take on relationships, and I could spot the subtle changes in her growth even though she couldn't.

I kicked myself for not having a first aid kit after I ran Beck's blood dried hand under tempered water. I patted her knuckles dry with a clean paper towel and apologized for not having bandages. When Beck was ready to go, I didn't press her to stay. I knew she had a lot to sort through in her head, and I was confident that she'd be back fairly soon. I made it my goal to have full bedding in place by the time she did.

The work progressed nicely with my house in the following weeks. I had replaced all the carpet with a light grey hardwood. Nearly all the smell left with the dead raccoon, and what had lingered was gone with the carpet. I spent my time working on the ruptured wall, while Beck went to school. Most days, she would come by in the evenings and help me with whatever project was on the list for that day. It was just how I imagined. We painted the bathrooms, and Beck decorated them in soft neutral colors. On the weekends, we spent hours in the dirt, planting flowers and getting sunburns. We cooked in the kitchen together, and she wore my T-shirts like tunics around the house. Slowly but surely, Beck began to feel comfortable in her Tethered skin.

Nearly a month had gone by when I said something that had shocked Beck. It never crossed her mind, and it seemed to have rattled her to her core. I wanted nothing more than to continue our forward momentum, but it was a look in her eyes that told me to tread lightly.

CHAPTER 20

"I'm . . . adopted!" Beck barked.

I stared up at her, dumbfounded, my jaw unhinged. I thought she knew. How could she not know? I lowered my paintbrush into the paint pan and tried to look anywhere but directly at her. The paint bucket was as good a place as any to wait it out.

"Seriously!? My mom and dad aren't my mom and dad?" Beck's mouth hung open. I knew she wasn't looking for an answer, so I steadied my course while the seconds ticked by. "Well, then who the hell is?" she asked.

Unlike me, Beck had parents. In fact, I saw one of them on the bridge just moments after she'd left me high and dry. Had she stayed just a little longer, we would have caused her father a lot of pain. His healing would have torn open like a fresh split on a scabbed knee. If Beck wanted to know her parents, there were stories I could tell her. Though that wouldn't ease her shock now.

The very first life I lived was under the roof of an

abusive family. I never had the chance to grow up. I never had the chance to see my fifth birthday. Once I got a couple of lives down the road, I learned that how I had grown up was anything but normal, and for the most part, parents weren't meant to be feared. I was a true lost soul. But Beck was different because even though she didn't remember her parents . . . I did. And they were everything a child could ask for and then some.

"I've got to call my mom! Or *whoever* she is!" Beck lowered off of the ladder and tossed her paintbrush in the pan, causing white paint to splatter my pants.

"Whoa, whoa, whoa! Are you sure you want to do that?" I asked.

"Why wouldn't I?"

"I don't know. It just seems like something you should think about first." I tried to save her from herself, but the woman was a damn tornado when she set her sights on something.

Beck beat her cellphone on the palm of her hand and paced the length of my living room. Fifteen minutes and one iced tea later, she slammed her glass down on the kitchen counter and declared a road trip.

"What?" I asked.

"I thought about it," she said.

"Well, that's—"

"I need to talk to my parents. And you're right, I should think about it first. I can do that in the car. It's nearly a six-hour road trip. That's plenty of time to figure out what to say or ask. God damn it, I should have seen the writing on the wall! Our parents were in that parenting group when we were young, and after you mentioned you were adopted, I realized that's what the group was for . . . I just never thought my parents were there for them. I imagined they were there to support your parents! God, I can be so dense sometimes!" Beck rambled on at the speed of light.

"No, don't say that. It's easy to overlook something when your heart steps in the way." Our minds played tricks on us all the time. Most people couldn't see anything clearly if they were emotionally wrapped up in it. And this was very emotional for a first-timer.

"I've got to go." Beck checked her watch. "I'll pick you up tomorrow morning?"

I smiled and nodded, not entirely convinced that come morning, she'd still want to confront her parents in person. I'd be by her side either way.

9:00 AM struck, and I was all but sure that Beck had given up on talking to her parents. Though that hadn't stopped me from packing a bag as soon as I woke, and it sat ready by the front door. I sipped my third cup of coffee, staring at my unfinished wall while I replayed her reaction over again in my head. I wondered if she would feel up to painting today after school; if she even made it, that was. If Becca was anything like Everly, she'd skip school and lay in bed wasting away. But what I was coming to believe was that Becca was a stronger version than the girl I had known before.

One hour and one fresh coat of paint later, a long honk

blared in my driveway. The low rumbling sound of bass grew before a car door slammed shut. I opened my front door, paintbrush in hand, to see Beck bounding forward with bright eyes and beautifully short shorts. "Aren't you supposed to be in school?" I asked.

"What do you mean? I thought we were going to see my parents?"

"Oh, yeah, of course! I just thought that maybe you would have changed your mind once you . . . had time to think about it some more." I set the paintbrush in the paint tray, and Beck took a step inside.

"Then what's that?" She pointed to my bag by the door.

I shrugged. "Proper planning?"

"Come on, let's go."

I looked around the tiny house with longing, but there was nothing here that couldn't wait a few days. "Give me a minute to lock up."

"OK, I'll be outside!" Beck said.

I hammered the lid onto the paint can and changed out of my construction clothes. When I stepped outside, the first thing I noticed was that Beck wasn't driving her truck. A black jeep sat eagerly in my driveway. The second thing I noticed was that Beck wasn't driving. Brooklyn was. I turned my back on the jeep and locked my front door, then swung my bag over my shoulder as I approached the back passenger's side. Brooklyn waved excitedly, and it was clear that I wasn't the only one who'd had three cups of coffee this morning. She and I hadn't talked since the day she accused me of "not knowing," whatever that had meant. But I could see by the smile on her face that it was water under the bridge. And if I was going to spend six hours with her in a car, I was happy to dismiss it as well. Just not forever.

I threw my bag into the back, wincing when I saw how much luggage had fit into Brooklyn's trunk. Not as much as they had packed for Las Vegas but similar. "I'm sorry, I didn't catch how long this trip was, and by the looks of your truck, I may or may not have . . . grey hair by the time I return," I said as I crawled into the back seat. I'd never understood the obsession of needing so many options. That is what was behind me, taking up half of the Jeep. It was shoes. I knew it. "Good morning to you too, Easton!" Brooklyn said.

"Good morning, Brooklyn." I shook my head, giving her an eye full of unfinished business.

Beck reached behind her seat to hand me a hot coffee they'd picked up while filling the vehicle full of gas. She shot me a glance that could only be described as *"I'm sorry,"* but I didn't mind. In fact, despite our last heated conversation, I thought Brooklyn was good for Beck.

"I'm not sure if you knew this, but Brooklyn and I went to high school together. So when we were looking at colleges, Brooklyn found Norton University and practically begged me to come with her." Beck rolled her eyes.

"I did not beg!" Brooklyn said.

"You did! She did." Beck nodded before turning back around, laughing.

"Wait, Brooklyn chose Norton?" I tried to read their faces, but the back seat did little in terms of view.

"It's where I'd always dreamed of going." Brooklyn

glanced into her rear-view mirror, fixing her eyes on me. They burrowed deep into mine, and though I couldn't read minds, I could read hers now.

"So we moved out here together and got an apartment close to the college. Anyway, long story short, she's going back to see her parents too. We've done this road trip a few times now and really have it down," Beck said.

I listened to the girls chat about a TV show. They were four seasons deep, and the drama ran as deep as the blue ocean. I stared out the window. When we crossed the New River Bridge, Beck busied herself by digging through her purse frantically. I leaned forward and gave her shoulder a squeeze, and she was so plagued with tension that it was contagious. I, too, became tense.

"Jesus Becca, what'd you forget?" Brooklyn said, trying both to keep her eyes on the bridge and look into Beck's bag for clues.

Beck threw her purse on the ground, and her eye caught on the window. I watched her reflection as she studied the bridge. I didn't know if it was the transparency of her eyes or true vacancy, but there was an emptiness in them. "Nothing," Beck said in a soft tone.

I sipped my coffee even though I was on the verge of being overstimulated and belted in place, no way to expel the energy coursing through my veins. I settled in for the long haul. Brooklyn filled the air with stories of high school Becca, and I wished I could reciprocate my favorite of the times we'd shared in the past. Then, when Beck couldn't withstand any more humiliation, Brooklyn switched gears to talk about her parents. They were both attorneys, and her brother was in law school. She called herself the black sheep of the family, and I wondered if that was the common thread between Beck and Brooklyn's friendship. Perhaps that was the reason I took so well to Brooklyn, too.

What should have only taken six hours would turn into an eight-hour road trip. Possibly longer. I learned more about Brooklyn in that time than I had ever aspired to, but I didn't mind. As much as the girls talked, and it was second to none, they never seemed to mention Beck's adoption. I gathered that Brooklyn wasn't yet privy to the information, and therefore, I kept my mouth shut. When the caffeine finally dissipated, my eyes drooped, and I fell into a dream like state of semi-consciousness.

The dream was nothing less than magnificent. The best part was, I was awake enough to control the outcome. Beck and I got to her parents' house, but they had taken off for a weekend getaway. We had the house to ourselves and treated it like a vacation, lounging around the pool and drinking her parents' liquor cabinets dry. I spent the days watching Beck under the sun and the nights admiring her new tan lines. One night, I convinced her to skinny dip with me. The water was chilly, but the hot tub was ready and waiting. I watched Beck undress as I stood naked by her side. Our toes breached the edge of the pool. I counted down from three with no intention of taking the polar bear plunge myself. Little did she know, I'd be getting her back for our bungee jump incident.

When I yelled three, Beck leapt into the pool, arms straight in the air and screaming until she hit the water with a splash. I stood at the pool edge bent in half laughing.

"Oh! Is he smiling?"

"What?"

"He is."

"Bet he's dreaming about you."

External whispers penetrated the boundaries of my dream, but nothing was more alluring than Beck's face when she came up for air to see me padding to the hot tub, dry as could be. I sank back into my subconscious, where Beck showed me just how angry she was with me in the sweltering hot tub. I awoke with a bump. My head slammed against the window.

"Ah!" I grabbed the side of my head and surveyed our surroundings. Brooklyn looked behind her seat and snickered. I pushed myself upright and wiped the drool that was seeping from my mouth while both girls laughed at me.

"Nice dream, Easton?" Brooklyn teased.

"Stop!" Beck sank into her seat.

"Very, very nice," I said. Both girls laughed with embarrassment, and heat rippled under my skin. Even with my eyes open, I could still see Beck enveloped in steam. I rubbed my eyes, trying to bring myself back to reality. Though it was the last thing I wanted to do.

"Well, we're about thirty minutes out."

"So, we'll be there in an hour?" I asked. Brooklyn's jaw dropped, but she had no comeback. I ran my hands through my hair and straightened my back, settling in for the last hour of the drive.

CHAPTER 21

$\mathcal{I}$t was dusk long before we met our destination and I had grown restless. I stretched my arms overhead, a groan escaping my throat. "Call me if you need anything. Love ya!" Brooklyn waved out the window as she drove away. I looked to Beck and then back at her parent's house. Not only was it massive, but it was dark, too. I was pretty sure that nobody was home.

"Did you tell them we were coming?" I asked.

Beck looked back at the house before pulling the handle out on her suitcase. "No, but I have a key."

"Well, are they going to be OK with you bringing a guy home?" I followed her to the large wrought iron doors.

"They don't care! They're going to be excited to see me . . . and they'll love you! You've got nothing to worry about." Beck pushed open the door and rolled her suitcase into the foyer, fumbling for the lights.

"Ahh . . ." A woman's muffled moan snapped us to attention. My pupils grew large, trying to cut through the darkness. My heart beat against my chest as I realized we had made a terrible mistake. Just as the lights flicked on, a naked woman rolled off the sofa and hit the floor with a thud. A man flailed his arms, spewing a long list of profanities as he covered his lap with a decorative throw pillow. The gold tassels swayed as the veins in his neck bulged. Beck cupped her mouth with both hands, dropping her bags to the floor. The suitcase handle slapped against the tile below, and the woman crawled on all fours behind the couch.

"What the fu—" Beck's dad hissed.

"Oh my god!" Beck squealed as she bolted out of the room, ultimately leaving me behind, staring at her naked father.

I had half the mind to reintroduce myself, but I wanted to make a good first impression. As slim as my chances were now—due to unforeseen circumstances—it didn't keep me from trying. I acknowledged him with a curt nod before making my slow exit. The panting and cursing faded as I ventured deeper into the house in my attempt to find Beck. I began to meander, though not aimlessly. I dragged my fingers across a full bookcase, catching a few titles I knew and loved. I admired some framed photographs of baby Beck in the hallway. Partially listening to the symphony of her parents' argument that played softly in the background. When I came upon the kitchen, it was obvious that we had come at a *really* bad time. Red roses unwound in a tall crystal vase, and the remembrances of mixed drinks lay on a wooden cutting board. Grains of salt and pools of lemon juice indicated a rushed mixing.

I briefly wondered if we'd be getting a hotel tonight when I heard a door slam and an echo in the distance. I still hadn't found Beck when her dad came upon me in the kitchen. His collar was popped and his pants were falling without the security of his belt. His face was nearly beet red. And if I hadn't known that Beck was adopted, I might say she'd gotten her complexion from him. I'd seen her flush like that more than a time or two.

"Who are you!?" he barked, still breathing heavily.

"Hello, sir. I'm Easton Green. Um, your old neighbor?" I reached my hand out, but he did nothing more than stare at it with cinched brows.

Beck's mom rounded the corner, wearing a white satin robe that hugged her body like a second skin. "Who are you? And where's Becca?" She tied her robe with a fierce double knot.

"Hi. I'm Easton Green, your old neighbor?" I extended my hand for the second time, and much like the first, she denied it too. She looked nothing like Beck with her dark features, and I was surprised that adoption had never occurred to Beck as a possibility before.

I pulled back my rejected hand and stuffed it into the pockets of my jeans, "I'm a—" I began, determined to make them like me.

"You know, maybe now is not the time. You should go," Beck's mom said. I had nowhere to go. My mouth fell open, but no words came out. The three of us waded through the awkwardness until Beck rounded the corner with a vengeance.

"What the fuck, Mom?" Beck said, holding her hand

high in the air. "Who the hell is *that!?*" she gestured to the man fidgeting with his belt.

What? Oh, no! My eyes darted from Beck to her father, not father . . . to her mother.

"Uhh, I'm going to get going, Lil," said the man. He hesitated for a moment before striding out of the kitchen.

"Does Dad know about this?" Beck hissed.

"Your father is away on a business trip," she said before giving me a long and uncomfortable gaze.

"You know, I should go too . . . I'm just going to go . . ." When my declaration had gone unnoticed, let alone unprotested, I followed the fool who'd walked out moments earlier.

I followed the man I'd thought to be Beck's second father outside but not before he collected his shoes from under the sofa. I took one last look into the house before I closed the wrought iron door, leaving the argument behind. "So what's your name, man?" I asked.

He studied me, scanning the length of my body. "Charlie," he said reluctantly.

"Hi, Charlie. I'm Easton," I said. The air had grown cooler, and the stars began to shine through the twilight sky. I took a seat on the curb while Charlie approached his car. With one foot on the floorboards of his car, he paused and looked me over one last time.

"Do you need a ride somewhere, kid?" he asked. I would have accepted if I had somewhere to go, but I didn't know this town from Adam. My time was best spent waiting it out on the curb. I hoped Beck would fetch me shortly.

"No, I'm OK. I'll be fine here. Thanks, though." Charlie gave me a quick nod before leaving, and soon I was left to my lonesome. I tried to adjust my seat, but no matter how I sat, the curb was uncomfortable. I spent the next half-hour watching the glowing lights flicker on and off in the surrounding windows—families watching TV—and trying to stretch my hearing as far as it could take me. When I thought they were finally done and it was safe to return inside, it would start up again. The rise and fall of the mother-daughter dispute finally ran its cycle, and I received a text from Beck asking me where I had been hiding.

Beck found me on the curb. I stood, letting her fall into my open arms. "I'm so sorry you had to see that," I said.

"Yeah. I'm sorry you had to see it too. Apparently, he was her art instructor," Beck said, and I couldn't be more grateful her head rest on my chest and she was unable to meet my gaze. I cleared my throat, buying myself time to gather a reply. "You know, I shouldn't even care. They're just two random people having sex. It's not like she's my mom anyway, right?" Beck pulled away to read my face.

"Well, I wouldn't go that far. I mean she raised you, right?" I said, and Beck sighed, letting a strand of hair twist around her finger. "Parents are the people who raise you. Sometimes, people have biological parents, and other times, it's who they learned under. It's about who made them feel safe and loved. Who taught them right from wrong. And sometimes, that may look more like a village than two people alone. I don't know, Beck. It's a perspective, I guess. I think you will have to just see what feels right when the dust settles." I shrugged, and a shiver rippled through my back. "It's cold out here. Are you warm enough?"

"Oh, yeah. Sorry. Let's go inside."

"What about your mom?" I asked.

"We won't even see her. Her room is on the opposite side of the house," Beck said as she pulled on my hand.

"Maybe we should get a hotel tonight. And however long we're planning on staying. I'm not confident I'm welcome."

"It's been such a long day, I just want to forget all about it," Beck said. I doubted that could happen with her mom still home, and despite the feeling that we were both invading her mother's privacy, I followed Beck back to the house. I kept my eyes peeled for white satin robe while Beck rummaged through the refrigerator, pulling out an assortment of meats and cheeses. She placed an apple, paring knife, and cutting board in front of me before looking through the cabinetry in search of crackers. I chopped the apple and assembled the charcuterie board that looked surprisingly appetizing for the short time it took to throw together.

Beck grabbed a bottle of wine before meandering into the backyard. "Let's eat out here. There are space heaters." I nodded and before picking up the charcuterie board. I gave a quick look around the kitchen, and when I was satisfied that I wasn't being watched, I stole a red rose from the crystal vase and spread the petals over our appetizer. I hoped the romantic touch would bring a smile to Beck's face.

I placed the cheese board on a table underneath the heater. Beck worked to get the heat burning, and I uncorked the wine. The backyard was beautifully manicured, and I admired the landscape and work that had been poured into it. "Did you want me to get some glasses for the wine?" I asked Beck. When the hot tub snagged the corner of my eye, my skin heated as I remembered my dream. Though just as quickly as it came, the memory turned from embers to ice as I realized that this weekend was anything but the one that I had dreamed up in my head.

"Nah, I don't mind drinking out of the bottle," Beck said.

"Oh. It's going to be one of those nights?" Beck rolled her eyes at my sarcasm and we both made ourselves comfortable in the lounge chairs underneath the heater. I started on the cheese and crackers while Beck got to work on the wine. She passed me the bottle, and I took a sip, careful not to spill.

"I just can't believe it. These people . . . I thought they were my parents, and now it's like I don't even know who they are. What's worse . . . I don't know who I am." Beck's stare sank to the bottom of the pool.

"I know who you are."

Beck looked at me. "Do you?" I began to nod, but Beck was more serious this time. "Seriously, you say that, but do you?"

"Well, yeah." I looked up into the sky briefly, confirming my answer. I knew I loved her. And I knew she had a large heart, a kind eye, and a loving touch. I knew my heart belonged to her. And I knew she was her own worst enemy. But would these things help her find her identity? Probably not. "I know your first parents. And your brother," I said.

"I had a brother?" Beck straightened, shock passing through her eyes.

I took another sip of wine and tried remembering how long it took me to regain my memory. "You really don't remember your brother?" I asked, passing her the bottle.

Beck shook her head and held the wine in her lap, tapping her nails against the glass. "I mean, I guess I do. Now that you say it, I feel like it must be true."

After a moment of silence passed between us, I leaned forward. "You should try the cheese. I think it's smoked Gouda." The smoke on my tongue danced with the red wine, and I was happy to eat nothing more than cheese for dinner underneath the warmth of the heater.

Beck smiled at me before dropping her gaze to the rose petal charcuterie board and frowned. "Did you steal my mom's roses?"

I froze, mid-chew. "What is wrong with you?" Beck asked.

I sucked in a piece of cracker and let out a barking cough.

Beck huffed. "You know you deserve that. Stealing roses from my mother's mans-tress . . ." Beck rolled her eyes at the ridiculousness of the situation, and I coughed up a cracker.

"It adds a romantic flare though, don't you think?" I said, still hacking.

Beck smiled and begrudgingly agreed. She loosened up just enough to try the smoked Gouda, causing her eyebrows to rise with surprised delight. "You know, if I close my eyes, I think I can see them, and I wonder if it's really my family, or just some fraction of make-believe I've conjured up in my head." Beck licked her fingers before wiping them on her jeans.

"God, I really wish there was something I could do to help you remember them. I mean, not just them but everything. I wish you remembered it all! What was it like when we were on the bridge? You seemed to remember once you were back in that specific location. Maybe we could, I don't know, imitate that by bringing you around town?" I asked.

"Yeah! Maybe? Do you think it could work?

"It already has, hasn't it?" I asked.

Beck tucked her hair behind her ears and wrapped her arms around her knees. "Kind of. When we were at the bridge, I felt . . . unsettled. The feeling gnawed at my stomach until I could no longer ignore it. Then, I saw your name on the memorial plaque, and I just lost it. In that moment, I knew that my intuition was correct and that, while I had thought I was crazy my entire life for feeling things I couldn't explain, finally, there was an answer. There was a plaque. I knew you were the secret's keeper, and I both blamed you for keeping it from me and needed you expediently."

"Lives," I said.

"What?" Beck looked to me, resting her cheek on her knees.

"You get to say *lives* now. Plural."

"Oh. Yeah. I guess." Beck directed her gaze to the stars above us, and I lowered my lounge chair so I could see them too. "I want to see them, Easton," she said in only a whisper.

"Who? Your family?"

"Yes. You have to take me to them."

"Oh, no, no, no. That's a big one, Beck. We can't do that."

"Why not!?" her voice rose.

"Beck, imagine you had a child. Now imagine you outlived that child. After twenty-one years of grief, you still wouldn't be healed. What do you think it would do to them if you suddenly came back into their lives? At the same age, no less! It's *not* fair to them."

Beck sat quietly for a long while, digesting my comments. "But I need closure too."

My stomach dropped. In my hundreds of years, I'd never thought about my own needs in the grieving process, and perhaps that's why I never healed myself. I briefly wondered if I'd even given anyone other than Beck the chance to touch my heart at all. I'd been so afraid of losing everyone I loved, I never even allowed my heart to open up.

My chest was heavy with regret, and I vowed to myself that I would take down my walls. I watched a small shooting star dart across the sky before fizzling out, and I brought my hand to my chest. My slow, methodical heart beat under my palm. Sometimes, I couldn't believe I was alive in the first place. I didn't know how I'd come to be

Tethered, but I knew that in that moment, I could do it better.

"I have a compromise for you to consider," I said after much thought.

"What's that?"

"We can stalk them."

Beck let out a stunted laugh. "What? Really? You want to *stalk* my parents?"

"It could be fun," I said, perching up on my elbow to look at her. "We can get binoculars and donuts, and we can sit in a stake-out car down the street from their house, waiting, for hours for them to check the mail. It will be nothing short of entertaining, and if we're lucky, it might help bring some of your memory back, too. Maybe you could get a little closure that way?" I reached over and took the bottle of wine from Beck's grasp.

"OK. Let's do it." Beck's tone was devoid of excitement, and I might have gone as far to say that it was a little annoyed.

"What is it? You don't think it will work?"

"Honestly?"

"Yeah, honestly."

"No. I don't think it will work."

"Why is that?" I asked.

Beck ran her hands through her hair in distress, causing my confusion to peak. "Because I don't remember you . . . and I've seen every inch of you."

I writhed in pain. The blow had been unexpected. I knew she was having trouble piecing everything together, but I hadn't known the extent of it. My jaw tensed as I watched the pool's surface ripple under the moonlight. This certainly wasn't the way I thought the weekend would go. "You don't remember me?" I asked in disbelief.

"Apart from your eyes, through the blood-stained water, and my lungs full of the icy river, I have no memory of you. Any of it, really." Beck's voice had run cold, and the vacancy behind her eyes had returned. No wonder she couldn't say she loved me back. The only part of me she remembered was the worst moment of her past life. My eyes were her grim reaper. I shut them tight, wishing she didn't feel pain every time she looked into them.

Our trip ended one day short. Beck's dad was coming home, and her mom didn't want us around when he did. Understandably, they had to talk. Beck never had her chance to sit down with her parents and ask them questions about the adoption. It was devastating for her to walk out the front door with no better sense of identity, but she clung to the hope that she would find herself through the lenses of binoculars on her old street. During our trip home, Beck told Brooklyn everything—aside from being cursed to walk the earth forevermore, of course. And after hours in the car, she had finally let go of some tension. Brooklyn even got her to laugh a bit, and for that, I was thankful.

I spent the rest of the road trip reflecting on my lives, dedicating myself to making Beck's life easier, happier, more enriched. That was the simple part. It was the poolside promise that I had made about loving without reservation that I'd need to work on. It was hard when everyone moved on and only I remained. It was hard to open up to the pain of saying goodbye. Especially when it wasn't a matter of *if* but a matter of *when*. But despite the inevitable hurt, I vouched to not only feel the broken hearts but the beating ones, too. I was going to love again.

I stopped at the donut shop before we got started. It was in every cop movie that featured a stakeout. And even though I'd had a plethora of career experience in my past, I never once considered being a cop. It was a real shame too, with my talent for regeneration. But could I live with all the crime at the end of the night? Was I strong enough to witness the corruption and the fate of the less fortunate? Could I then knock on homes of the unknowing? Could I continue to fight, through the thick of it, without letting it destroy me from the inside out? I'd like to think so. I steepled my fingers under my chin as I wondered if I could pass the physical entry test.

"You want this one?" The lady behind the glass window pointed to a pink sprinkled donut.

"Um, sorry, yes I'll take one of those, and a powdered one, and two cronuts please." I dug in my pocket for cash as I pictured myself as a police officer. I couldn't quite put my finger on why it didn't look right in my head, and I shook the image away when the clerk asked if I wanted coffee.

"Two, please."

"That will be $8.89."

I handed the clerk a ten and placed a couple of bills in her tip jar. I picked up Beck from her apartment, leaving the donuts in the car but taking the coffees with me. The warmth from the cups were a welcome contrast to the brisk air against my knuckles. It felt nice to be near campus again, as I had avoided it in my attempts to finish the renovation of my house. After I climbed the stairs to Beck's apartment, I kicked the door lightly with my foot, trying not to spill the coffees in my hands.

Brooklyn opened the door in short shorts and a crop top. She crossed her arms attempting to hide her chest as she called for Beck. "Becca! Easton is here! Oh . . . Is that for me?" Brooklyn asked, lashes lifted.

"Uh, yeah!" I looked down at the coffees, trying to remember which one I had been drinking out of, but when I couldn't recall, I handed her the left one.

"You're so sweet! Thank you!" I gave her a quick nod, my gaze lingering while I searched for what she claimed to know better than me. "Where are you guys off to?" Brooklyn said, sipping my coffee.

"We're having a picnic," I said.

"A breakfast picnic?"

"Exactly." Brooklyn's eyes lowered to half-mast as she realized she wasn't the only one with secrets.

Beck was quick, and I'd have to wait for another time to finish my conversation with Brooklyn. She didn't appear as worried as I was. Beck grabbed her bag before giving me a quick peck on the cheek. She took the coffee from my hand and waved Brooklyn goodbye with her pinky finger. "I have donuts and binoculars," I said.

"I brought a trucker hat and oversized sunglasses!" I laughed, realizing that I typically had those things in my car, ready at all times. "I'm really nervous." Beck tried to smile through a clenched jaw.

I stalled and pulled Beck in for an embrace. "You have nothing to be nervous about. We probably won't even get a sighting. Not for a few days, anyway."

Beck pulled away, and her brows stitched together.

"I mean, we're totally going to see them. We're going to see them so hard!" I smiled and slapped the bill of Beck's hat, tipping it down to the bridge of her nose.

She smiled her pearly whites and lifted the hat to see again. "Now that's the spirit! Let's go stalk some old people!" Beck said.

We got in the car, and I made my way to Clover, trying everything I could to make Beck wait for the donuts until we were in position, but she didn't understand my vision and swallowed the pink one nearly whole. "They're such a treat! I never eat these!" she said through a mouthful of pink glaze.

"I can see that!"

"What are these brown ones? They look . . . incredibly boring." Beck stared into the box, hunting for her next kill.

"Uh, those are the best ones! They're a mix between a croissant and a donut. You have to at least try it. Not now, though. Just wait."

Beck did as I asked, and I laughed every time I saw her eyes flicker back to the box. It wasn't until I pulled into her old neighborhood that my excitement shifted and I became apprehensive of the whole plan. There were so many things that could go wrong . . . and so few that could go right. "Do you recognize any of this?" I tried to capture Beck's expression, but her head was turned away, looking out the window. If only the back of her head could talk.

"I don't know? I mean, it looks like every other neighborhood, doesn't it?"

"True. But if you had to say which house on this street was yours, which one would you choose?"

Beck looked to both sides of the street before leaning forward in her seat. Her hands gripped her seat and her knuckles were taught and white. I drove slowly, allowing her time to look at each one in thoughtful deliberation. My heart fluttered at the sight of her house, but I tried to remain unbiased. "Well, if I had to choose, I'd say that one with the little bushes that lead up to the front door."

I don't know why it shocked me that she was right, but it did. "What makes you think it's that one?" I asked.

Beck looked at her other options and then back to her old home. "I can't say for sure, it's not anything in particular. Just a feeling. A draw."

"A tether?" I asked.

Beck turned her head slowly and looked into my eyes, "That's *exactly* how it feels. Look!" She raised her arm between us, and it was covered in goose flesh. The tiny hairs on her arm were standing straight up.

I grabbed her hand and kissed the back of her knuckles,

which were nearly healed from her demolition mishap. "You're right. That's it."

Beck nodded, taking it in. I parked on the opposite side of the street, making sure our view was the best it could be without being too obvious. I looked to Beck who was no longer consumed with the pastries, and I handed her the large sunglasses to hide behind. I pulled my old trusty cap on and we sat in silence, staring at the house. After ten minutes or so, I reached for the box of donuts. I bit into a cronut while I held the binoculars up to my eyes and tried to peer through every window of the house. If someone was home, I couldn't tell. "I think I might want to try being a cop," I said.

Beck let out a snort. "Yeah. You should do that."

I turned to her, but her face was no more than a blur. I lowered the binoculars slowly. "You laughed," I stated.

"No . . . there was something in my throat." Beck rubbed her throat, reminding me of the way she did when she had cancer.

"You literally snorted."

"No, I just think, you know . . . if you're going to be a cop that maybe you should start lifting weights or something. Maybe."

I stared at her, unable to see her eyes through large tinted sunglasses. Her thin pressed lips were all I needed to know that she was stifling a giggle.

"Are you saying I'm not masculine enough to be a cop?"

Beck slid her glasses down the bridge of her nose and peered up at me with her large green eyes. "Honey, that's precisely what I'm saying."

My jaw unhinged, and my eyes grew with wild delight. "You!" I ripped my seatbelt off, "Little!" I began to crawl over to the passenger's seat and Beck squealed. My head hit the ceiling, and my knees kicked into my chest. My foot caught the center console, and my hands grabbed fistfuls of Beck to steady myself. She screamed, much too loud for a stake-out. It was a rookie move. Fully on top of her, I reached down, fumbling to find the seat recline lever. "Say it. Say I can be a cop!" When her mouth glued shut, I ripped the lever, and we both fell flat against the reclined seat. Beck laughed so hard her face turned red and a vein bulged in her neck. She looked just like her mother's art instructor. I showed no mercy, jabbing my fingertips into her ribs and blowing puffs of air into her ear. She squealed like a boar and fought like one too.

In my attempts to seek revenge, I hadn't even noticed a woman approaching Beck's window. Two knobby hands pressed against my tinted window, making binoculars of their own. Eyes of papier mâché peered down at us. Who knew how long she had been watching? Beck hissed at me when I rolled my window down. "What are you doing?"

"Can I help you, ma'am?" I asked. The lady was appalled by either our display of affection or the fact that she had gotten caught—which one I couldn't tell. She muffled some inaudible words under her breath before walking away, her wiener dog trotting behind her. I opened Beck's door and nearly fell out of the car. I got up, dusting off my clothes, stood to my full height, and walked back to the driver's seat in stride. The lady shot me several dirty looks over her shoulder. And by the last look of utter distaste, I wondered what she truly thought was happening in the parked car.

"Do you think she's going to call the *real* cops? You know, the ones with muscles?" I asked Beck.

"Jesus, you can't let anything go, can you?" Beck was amused by my sarcasm, which only made me want to lay it on thicker.

"Too bad we don't have a dog to walk. If we did, we could get closer." I regretted it the moment I said it. Something in the way Beck's eyes sparkled screamed *mischief*, and I wasn't sure I was up for it.

"I've got a . . . compromise."

I didn't like the way she said it. "No."

"Wha—"

"No."

Two hours later, Beck and I stood at her parent's front door wearing navy blue jumpsuits and face coverings. Beck insisted on holding a clipboard, and I made her promise that under no circumstances would she speak. She rapped on the front door, and nerves coiled in my stomach. It was the very moment I tried to avoid, and here I was, against my better judgment, knocking on the door. I prepared my opening line about needing to test for termites. I'd use several of the neighbors as referenced clients. But when nobody answered the door, I was relieved. Though, relief was quickly chased away by a more powerful, gut-wrenching anxiety when I turned to Beck to see no sign of disappointment in her expression. The twinkling in her eyes told me I was in for much worse than a knock on the door.

"What are you trying to do to me?" I hissed as she tiptoed through the boxwood bushes toward the backyard.

"Quiet!" Beck hissed as she tried to open the first window she came upon. I knew right then and there I'd be spending the night hiding in the pantry with her.

"Beck, seriously, we can't get caught!" I followed her to the slider, and her eyes grew with excitement when the door rolled down the tracks, which officially meant breaking and entering. I let out a trapped breath, as I knew I'd do just about anything to make her happy. "OK . . . but get closure and then get out!" It was my only stipulation—that we do it quickly.

"Closure. Got it." Beck disappeared into the house and the drapes sucked outside, blowing into the mid-morning air. I pushed through them, following her blindly. My eyes searched the house frantically while they adjusted to the dim shadows. It looked similar to what I'd remembered. And at least I knew it was the right house and her parents hadn't moved. That would have been a different kind of disaster—one that I wasn't prepared for.

Beck moved quickly, making her way to a large hutch covered in framed photos. She stilled when she found a picture and pulled it close to examine. I wanted nothing more than to comfort her in that moment, but the thought of getting captured on videotape consumed my thoughts. I scanned the room for small red lights and anything that blinked. I couldn't imagine how her parents would feel watching their daughter's ghost rummage through their house, and I didn't want to be haunted by the thought.

It wasn't until I caught a tear rolling down Beck's cheek that I stopped looking for security cameras and came to be by her side. "We were married?" she whispered. Her hands gripped the picture frame tightly as if it might slip away at any moment. "Why didn't you tell me!" Her whisper turned to a hiss.

"I . . . I was going to—"

"You seriously just pretended to be my neighbor . . . when you were really my *husband*!?" This wasn't a whisper at all. She was furious. But this hardly seemed like the right time to discuss it, as we stood in the dark home we had broken into.

"It . . . it was a delicate situation!" She had to know that.

"You let me get screwed over by Nolan, knowing damn well that I loved you!? That I'd already found my match? You just stood by the wayside letting me make mistake after mistake?"

"How was I supposed to know you would choose me again? I honestly didn't think you could love me twice. I had no choice but to let you choose on your own terms!" I said in a hasty yet hushed voice, still aware of our surroundings even though she was not.

She swiped the tear from her cheek and tucked the picture of us on our wedding day under her arm. It was the one where I planted kisses all over her face and she tilted her head back in exquisite loving laughter. I remembered the moment like it was yesterday.

"Wait, what are you doing? You can't take that!"

"Why?"

"Beck! Seriously? Take a picture with your cellphone or something, but leave that here!" I begged.

Beck sighed, giving me a look that could set fire to rain-soaked logs. She placed the picture down on the hutch and pulled out her cellphone. Hastily, she snapped photos of every picture she could before following me to another room. "Which room was mine?" Beck asked.

"I don't know. You didn't live here when I met you." We opened every bedroom door, peaking in quickly. But before Beck could shut the master bedroom door, there was something that caught her eye, rendering her motionless. "What is it?" I asked. When she didn't answer, I began to worry. I pushed the bedroom door open, and Beck walked inside. "What did you find?" I whispered, searching for red blinking lights.

Beck didn't answer, and I was suddenly pulled in a different direction than she. I took one last look at her as she approached the dresser, and I turned my focus to the nightstand. There was something about being a Tethered Soul that allowed you to know without reason. The draw was so deeply embedded in my chest. It was like an anchor digging into the ocean floor. I stepped up to the nightstand, pulled the top drawer open, and lifted the small box from within. I didn't need to open it to know what was inside, but my eyes couldn't survive coming so close and not witnessing it one more time. I opened the box, and Beck's first wedding ring sparkled—even through the bedroom shadows.

A car door slammed. Then another. The sound was so

close, it had to be in the driveway. We froze, twisting to see each other and hoping someone had an answer. But neither of us was prepared for this. My feet felt heavy like I was sinking into quicksand. My mind raced. We didn't spring into action until keys entered the front door, at which point full-blown panic ensued. On pure instinct, Beck grabbed my hand, leading me to the master bathroom. She closed the door behind us and worked to open the small window that led to the side yard. I realized I still had the ring in my hand and as much as I knew I should, I wasn't able to let it go. I thrust it into my pocket before boosting Beck up so she could climb out the tiny window. When it was my turn to squeeze through, I was thankful for my lean build. Had I been any stronger, I might not have fit at all.

I slid down the wall, the stucco scrapping my palms as I tried to find gripping. Hanging half way out the window, I was about as graceful as a fawn still learning its footing. I fell to the bushes below with a thud, leaving one shoe behind in the restroom. I scrambled to my feet and peered into the window at the lone shoe in the middle of the floor. There was no way I could retrieve it in time.

"Let's go!" Beck hissed.

"My shoe?" I tripped on my way out of the bush, falling onto my knees.

"Leave it! Let's go!" Beck took off, running to the car, her back half-hunched. I looked back at the window, knees and palms pressed into the wet lawn. I took off after her, limping with one shoe, and one wet sock. We slammed our doors shut. "Go! Go! Go!" Beck wailed, and I peeled out. My heart was beating against my chest like a butterfly trapped in a glass jar. I flew around the corner onto the main road and blew through a yellow light, speeding down the straightaway.

In reality, it would probably be hours before Beck's parents went to draw a bath and noticed the shoe, and even then—at their age—they might just place it back into the closet without a second thought.

By the time we were some way down the main road and my speed had slowed, Beck and I began to laugh. My anxiety lifted, and the high of the thrill took hold. "I can't believe my shoe came off!" I said, and Beck snorted. "And did you see me squeeze through that tiny window? How's that for being manly? If I had been twenty pounds heavier, I wouldn't have made it out alive!" I claimed.

Beck grinned. "Yeah, you're a real modern-day Cinderella . . ."

CHAPTER 23

We hid the getaway car inside my garage. After hunkering down, Beck and I ordered Chinese food for delivery. Still riding the wave of adrenaline, I was saddened that Beck didn't feel the same way. I wanted to celebrate a victory, but she was anything but victorious.

"Do you mind if I stay the night?" Beck asked.

"Stay the night? Beck, you can stay the night every night for the rest of your life! Quite frankly, I've been a little surprised that you haven't moved in with me already." She forced a smile. "What is it?"

"Move in with you?" Beck's eyes grew with shock.

"Well, you *are* my wife," I said cautiously.

"*Was* your wife."

I swallowed the lump in my throat and nodded in agreement. "I'm sorry I didn't tell you earlier. I want you to know, I thought about you every day. And after I finally found you, you seemed so happy that I questioned if I was right for you, this time. I wanted to tell you, but I was afraid," I said.

"Afraid of what?"

"That it would be too much, too soon. That having a past life would upset you. That you wouldn't love me like you promised."

"So you kept it to yourself?"

"No! I let you choose. I let you ask. It's different! I'm sure I could have done it better, but I tried my best to not interfere with your decisions and memories. And you chose me! Again! Without even knowing you had before. Don't you think that's invaluable for us to know?"

Beck closed her eyes, and when she opened them, they took on a warmth that was previously absent. She nodded. "I'm sorry for being upset. It's just a lot to take in. I don't want any more secrets between us, OK?"

"None?" My eyes darted to the corners of the room. I had a lot of secrets and a lot of lies. So much so, sometimes I wondered what was true and what was fiction.

"Easton!" Beck popped a hand on her hip.

"I love you," I said cowering.

Beck sighed, opening her mouth but ultimately closing it without repeating the words back. She hadn't said it yet, and I was starting to worry. "Come here," I said, holding my arms out. She wrapped her arms around me and pressed her ear against my chest.

"I can hear your heart beating," Beck said.

I rested my chin on the top of her head and sighed.

"It's just, I went looking for closure, but now, I think I'm too afraid to get it."

"What do you mean? Are you afraid to look at the pictures you took?" I asked.

Beck pulled away from my grip. "No. I'm afraid to read these." She lifted a stack of journals from her bag. They were tied tight with a large burlap bow. My stomach dipped, realizing I wasn't the only one who stole something from our last life.

"What are those?" I asked.

Beck's eyes began to water, and she looked anywhere but directly at me. "I recognized them. They're mine!" Beck said defensively.

"Beck you can't! You shouldn't have! I never should have let you—" I stopped myself there, knowing that I, too, was guilty of meddling in her parents' lives. I left a shoe on their bathroom floor, for God's sake. I scrubbed my eyes and exhaled long and deep. The doorbell rang.

"But they're mine . . ." Beck said.

"I know," I said, the ring burning a hole into my leg. With a frown, I turned to answer the door. Our Chinese had arrived. I thanked the delivery kid and brought the bag of food into the kitchen.

"I know . . . Maybe you should read them, and then we can put them back?" I nodded, devising my plan. I couldn't bear the thought of breaking back into the house, but it was the only answer I could come up with. "Do you think it will help you to remember?"

"I don't see why they wouldn't. I remembered that they were mine. I just knew without a shadow of a doubt. But, if I'm honest, a part of me doesn't want to remember. When I saw the picture of us, it made me feel sick inside. How could I marry a man and forget him? When I saw these journals, I knew they were the answers to all my questions. The only thing I don't know is . . . am I strong enough to read them?" Beck said as she tucked a strand of her hair behind her ear.

"I could read them to you?"

"No! I mean, no, I can do it by myself. I just need a little space and time," Beck said.

"Well, make yourself comfortable. I can build a fire, and you can settle in with a blanket and read your past memories."

After dinner, we did just that. I built a fire and Beck began to read. She started with her first journal, the one she wrote when she was a child. Judging from the amusement on her face, I imagined it was going well for her. I busied myself setting the new tile backsplash in the kitchen while Beck made random sounds from the living room. Every now and again, I'd steal glances at her, curious what she'd uncovered. I was eager for her to get to the part where she met me, and I wondered if she would let me read it.

An hour later, I was halfway through the mosaic and Beck was onto her second journal. Her amusement began to lessen, and by the time she was a few pages into the third book, tension had soiled the air. Her face was lit by the glow of the fire, and her tears were highlighted with the dancing flames. Nothing would have made me feel better than to rush to her side and promise that everything would be OK. Wash away the pain of old memories with my kisses. But she didn't need that. She needed space. And time. Two things that proved to be challenging for me.

I ended up taking a deck of cards to my bedroom and shutting the door to give her privacy. I knew she wouldn't have that back at her apartment with Brooklyn, so I tried my best to give her what she needed here. I practiced counting cards until the early hours of the morning as I listened to muffled sounds come from Beck in the living room. When some time had passed in silence, I went out to check on her. She lay on the sofa with the journal opened across her chest and pink swollen eye sockets. She must have cried herself to sleep. I pulled the blanket over her and threw another log on the fire before going to bed myself, though I wouldn't sleep soundly.

When morning came, Beck was gone and so were the journals. The blanket had been tossed to the floor. Worry spread through me as I checked the front yard and saw my car missing. But when I hurried into the kitchen, a note was taped onto the coffee pot dispelling my concerns. Beck was at school. And the fact that she was well enough to go to class told me that everything was going to be alright. Perhaps it would be even better than alright.

I grew excited for the possibility that Beck had finally found herself. Her identity uncloaked. I couldn't wait to look into her eyes and see my girl. The one I had fallen in love with on the bridge. Sure, she was the same person, and I had been looking into the same green eyes for months now, but I'd been searching those emerald flecks for recognition. And that was something I had missed deeply. I picked up Beck's ring and slid it into my pocket, unsure if the time would come for me to give it to her. But I'd rather be ready than not, and I was hopeful.

I called a taxi to drive me to Norton University. The sky was bright and cloudless, and I couldn't help but think it was the perfect day to welcome Beck back home. Being with Beck . . . her memory and all . . . That was my dream come true. And I never would have imagined it was so important until it wasn't there. A whole life erased. The secrets we shared. The things we said, and the things we didn't. The living we did while we were alive. The moments we shared before we weren't. It was a bigger part of who we were than I had realized. Beck knew she loved me, but without her memories, she didn't know *why*. And maybe that was why she hadn't admitted it. Maybe today was the day.

When I arrived at the college, I bought a coffee from a vendor on campus and waited for Beck under the oak tree. My tree.

I waited with all the patience in the world. The wait was almost euphoric with anticipation. I listened to the chatter within earshot about weekend plans and test grades. The birds chirped in the oak tree, and a gentle breeze blew by, rustling the leaves. I ran my hand through the damp grass and my back went rigid when I felt what I knew to be a diamond ring under my fingertips. Slowly, I plucked it from the blades of grass. It was in perfect condition, no gouges from a lawnmower sucking it up and spitting it out. The diamond still sparkled as it did in the jewelry shop months ago. I dug into my pocket and pulled out the original wedding band to compare them side by side. They were different, slightly, and the original was a little misshapen, having been pulled from the wreckage.

As I looked over the two rings, the past and the present, I grew unsure of which ring to give to Beck. "What have you got there?" Brooklyn asked, startling me. I nearly dropped both rings into the sea of grass, never to be found again. I shoved them in my shirt pocket, hopeful they would be safer there. Brooklyn eyed me with her golden eyes and one lifted brow.

"Hey, Brooklyn. Have you seen Beck today?"

"No, she didn't come to school today. In fact, she didn't come home last night. Is everything alright?"

I patted my pocket, causing both rings to jingle. "Oh, yeah, everything's fine. I just thought she was at school today, so I dropped by to have lunch with her. Have you heard from her at all today?" I asked.

Brooklyn took a seat next to me and then checked her phone. "No, I haven't, but uh . . . Did I see a ring in your hand?"

I looked to Brooklyn, caught red-handed, and I couldn't help but smile. "Maybe."

"You're really going to do it?" Brooklyn looked unsure of how she felt about it.

"Yeah, I really am." I pulled out one ring, it didn't matter which one my fingers found first, and I handed it to her. It was the new band.

"Wow, Easton, she's going to love it!"

"Think she'll say yes?" I joked.

"Well, yeah. How could she not?" Brooklyn handed the

ring back. I eyed her suspiciously. Brooklyn shrugged, "What?"

"What do you mean, how can she not? She has a choice . . ." I had made sure of that.

"I know that. It's just, you guys are kind of fated, though, right? Do you really think you have a choice when it comes to fate?"

I looked into her eyes, trying to read between the lines. "Fated?"

"You know, you said she was your soulmate and your puzzle piece—all of that sappy stuff." Brooklyn rolled her eyes and began to gather her things.

"Wait, but you were the one who said—"

"I'm sorry, Easton. I've got to run. I don't want to be late for class. Good luck!" Brooklyn said.

"Brooklyn, wait!" I said, catching her by the wrist. "Wait!" She spun, her eyes meeting mine. "Talk to me," I begged.

Brooklyn sighed, letting the fight escape with her breath. "OK. I . . . I sometimes have these dreams."

She stopped there, as if it were enough to answer my rising suspiciousness about her. "And?" I let her arm go, and she rubbed her wrist mindlessly.

"And, they sometimes come true."

"Sometimes?" I asked.

"*All* the time."

"Do you get these dreams often?" I asked.

"I've always gotten them. But not many know, so you can't say anything to anyone. Not even Becca."

"I won't," I promised before knowing if I was able to

keep it. Brooklyn frowned. "Did you have a dream about her?"

"I've had a dream about the two of you, and it didn't end well." Her eyes creased, and she looked to the ground.

"And by that you mean?" I pushed her to continue.

"I mean, you two didn't make it."

"Like, we split up?" I asked, dreading the worst.

Brooklyn let out a stunted laugh that was anything but funny. "No, like you guys died," she said, worry lining her forehead.

I almost burst into laughter but fought to contain myself. Here I thought that Beck wouldn't accept my proposal, but it was only death. That, we had done before, and we would continue to do it a thousand times over. Poor Brooklyn, she had been worried about a premonition, but little did she know, it was already in the past.

"Well, if you're so worried about us dying, then why have you been trying to pair us up?" I asked.

"I can't control my dreams. They just kind of will me down a particular path, and then once I'm there, they take on a new form. I knew that she was meant to be with you. Not that asshole Nolan. But it wasn't until more recently that I saw your death," Brooklyn said.

"Look, I appreciate you telling me this. But I don't want you to worry over nothing," I said, placing a hand on her shoulder.

"It's not nothing," Brooklyn said.

But I couldn't explain it to her. She was now the one who didn't understand. And while I thought her ability to dream of reality was neat, I had a wife to find. "Of course not. I'll be very careful. Thank you for looking out for us. You're a good friend." Brooklyn bit her lip, looking like she could go on for days about her dreams. "I've got to go find Beck, I'll catch you later," I said, and she nodded reluctantly before heading to class.

There, under the shade of the tree, I stood stranded and slightly sidetracked. I called Beck's phone again to no avail. Where would she go if she had remembered everything? What would she do? A thought sparked, and I was on the phone calling another taxi. I had to get to the ridge of the Truly River.

I waited for my ride in the parking lot, where I had spotted Nolan talking to a girl by his truck. She was neither Beck nor Payton, but a third prospect. Long black hair that touched her waist and highlighted her bare skin between jeans and crop top. Nolan's stance was wide, encapsulating her between his legs. He pulled out his phone as she did hers, and I presumed they exchanged phone numbers. I wondered where his relationship stood with Payton, but when my ride rolled through the parking lot looking for the rideless, my attention fell back to my missing girl.

I watched the perfect day pass by through the cab window and hoped my inclination was right about where Beck had run off to. When the cab pulled up to our old campsite and I saw my car parked at the mouth of the hiking trail, I finally got the relief I'd been waiting for.

I thanked the cab driver and walked up to my car, placing a hand on the front hood. The car was cold and therefore had been parked for some time. I set off, jogging down the trail, eager to meet my bride. The pines passing by and tall damp grass nipping at my calves. A slow burn spread across my chest as my heart worked to keep up with my pace. Once I reached the clearing, I could see Beck there at the cliff's edge. The wildflowers danced in the field between us, and Beck's hair looked alive, set to motion by a cool gust. Every step closer was a step closer to my fate, and I could feel that I had nearly grasped the brightly burning star that I'd once wished upon so long ago.

CHAPTER 24

$\mathcal{I}$ walked through the field, my hand over my shirt pocket. The rings clamored together, past and present clashing. Beck turned around and offered me a slight smile, though it didn't reach her eyes. I wrapped my arms around her waist and rested my chin on top of her head. I said nothing. The view from where we stood was astonishing and grounding all at once. If you came here to look down at the Truly River not knowing who you were, you would at least leave knowing who you *wanted* to be.

"You found me," Beck said softly. I squeezed her tight. That I had.

"You remember. Beck, I've waited so long for this moment. I love you. I've loved you through sickness and health. Through life and death and back again." I reached into my shirt pocket and lowered down onto one knee. The ring I grabbed was the original, and it shined brightly under the ray of the sun. Beck turned around, stunned to see my intention. "Will you make me the happiest man and be my wife . . . again? Now, and forever?"

Beck brought her hand to her mouth, leaving me to read her eyes alone. Her tears left me guessing for far too long, and my heart nearly exploded out of my chest in anticipation of her reply. "Beck, say something," I begged.

"It's coming back . . . slowly. You know how you can look at a picture of yourself as a kid, and you smile and say 'I remember that,' only you don't—you remember the picture? It's like that. I read my journals, and I remember, but it's like I only remember what I wrote. I understand how I felt, but somehow it doesn't translate. I don't feel that way now. It's not the same, Easton, I was a different person then. It was—"

"A lifetime ago?" I asked.

"Yes. That's exactly it." Beck's eyes were filled with sadness and marked with doubt. I found them to be contagious.

My gaze dropped to the ring in my outreached hand. Had she not felt the same way about me now? Beck lowered to her knees and sat back on her heels, taking the ring from me, but not placing it on her finger. I sat down, defeated. "Beck, do you still love me?" It was the only question that mattered now.

"That's the thing, Easton. I do love you . . . but is that because I remember I did? Is it because I'm supposed to?" Beck ran her finger down the dent in the ring, and I watched as the sparkle of the diamond dimmed as her face fell. "I almost feel like I'm stuck between two people. I don't know who I am anymore! But if I know one thing . . . I'm not her. I'm not Everly Beck." Beck handed the ring back to me abruptly as if the pain of having it was too much.

"But you *do* love me?"

"Yes." Beck grabbed my hand.

"Say it?" I asked. "I need to hear it. I've waited so long to hear it."

"Easton, I *love* you. I just—"

"Stop! That's all I need," I said. I couldn't take what was coming out of her mouth next. And I still needed the first part to sink in.

I took the other ring out of my pocket and stared down at it for a moment before handing Beck my heart of glass. I knew I was asking a lot, but I couldn't live with the regret if she left me now. "I want to be with you. Beck. Becca . . . The first life, the tenth . . . It's all the same to me. It's natural to be scared. But you don't have to do it alone anymore. I'll be here for you whether or not you put this ring on your finger. I just want you to know that."

"What's that?" Beck asked. I looked at her as she stared into my hand holding not one but two diamond rings. "Why are there two?"

I shook my head, nearly giving up. "I'm a lost soul, Beck. What more can I say? You know, before I met you, I thought I had it all figured out. I'd go about my life, trying to make other people happier. I thought I would brighten the world one Sue at a time, and it worked for a while . . . but then you came along, and everything changed. I found balance when I found you. Everything hurt more deeply, but the love you showed me was well worth the pain, and more. You took down my walls, and I never want to build them again. You're the center of my universe, Beck, but if you want to know who you are . . . you're so much more than that!" I watched Beck melt before me as my words struck a chord with her, and the green in her eyes softened to match the grass. "Let me ask you this, Beck: who do you *want* to be?"

Beck picked a wildflower and pinched off the purple petals one at a time, entranced in thought. "Well, I can tell you who I don't want to be," she said.

"OK then . . ."

"I don't want to be that girl I used to be. The one who thought life was . . . cruel. But I don't want to be the girl I am now either! The one who's too afraid to try!"

"Beck, you have all the time in the world to craft who you want to become. Learn the lessons you need. The hand you've been dealt is nothing more than chance. But it was you who chose to deal with it bravely, and that's been a choice. Nobody can take that from you. I know you won't believe me when I say this, but I've already seen incredible growth from you. I can't wait to see the person you blossom into . . . if you let me."

Beck plucked her last petal. "He loves me," she murmured. A smile spread across her face. "I'm just scared."

"I know." I reached over and lifted the hem of her shirt.

"What are you doing?" Beck squirmed.

"Let me see it?" I asked.

"See what?"

"The twig."

Beck's mouth fell open. "What? Why?"

"It's literally the epitome of your fear. Come on!" I laughed. Beck rolled her eyes and lifted her shirt, baring a cat scratch in black ink across her ribs. I covered my mouth, laughing into my hand. Beck's eyes sparkled, and I could see that the fear no longer held her back.

"Seriously, though, why do you have two rings?" A small amused laugh escaped her.

"I thought . . . that the second I found you, you would bound into my arms. I'd kiss you a thousand times and when you finally let go, I would lower onto one knee and propose. I thought we would pick up right where we left off," I shook my head at my stupidity.

"And we lived happily ever after," Beck smiled and flicked the flower stem away.

"Yeah. That's exactly what I thought."

"That's so sappy!"

I laughed at her bluntness, and the embarrassment caused my face to warm. I guess I was a hopeless romantic. I never gave it much thought. I glanced at her and she winked at me. My heart lurched in my chest. "Yeah. Pretty fucking stupid!" I said, and both Beck and I burst into laughter, letting all the tension fade between us. She shoved me and I flinched before grabbing her and pulling her into me. She fell against my side and inched lower to rest her head in my lap. Her giggles trailed off, and she looked up to the sky. I dug a palm into the grass behind me.

"This reminds me of grey skies and rainfall . . . a slow, tender dance. And if I close my eyes tight enough, I can almost taste the champagne on my lips." Beck smiled with her eyes sealed. The sun beamed down on her face, allowing her skin to shine almost ethereally.

Her memory was painted not only with her words but in the smile on her face. It was almost real—like I could taste it too if I just closed my eyes. "Beck? That memory wasn't written in your journals," I said. Beck's face compressed under the sun, and a stream of fresh tears ran into her hair. When she opened her eyes, she didn't need to confess her love for me or place a ring on her finger because I could see it not only in her but all around her. Like fireflies glowing and gleaming in the air, tucked between blades of grass and tangled in her pale blond hair.

"Easton, I don't know what I would do without you. I may have a lot of self-discovery left to do, but I'm my best self when I'm with you. I love you, and I want to spend the rest of my life with you. Not only our past life. Not only this one. But the future ones too. I'm all in. It's you and me, OK?" Beck let her tears run freely as she gazed up at me, her eyes full of love and promise.

My heart mended back together, stronger than it was before it had broken. Beck chose me. *Again.* And it wasn't because she was down and out or because she had no other choice. She chose me because I'd won her heart, and she'd have it no other way. "It's us against the world," I said.

Beck snickered as the tears fell. She nodded in agreement. "You and me." "Which ring do you want?" I asked.

Beck sat up, placing a finger to her lips. "I want the first one—the original. It's been through a lot, and I'm not done with that girl yet." Beck smiled widely and held out her left hand. I glided the ring onto her finger. Despite the dent, it still fit her perfectly. She held it out for both of us to admire. I took her hand in mine and kissed it.

"I have a safe deposit box I can send the other ring to for safekeeping."

"You mean, for another life?" Beck asked.

I wiped her tears away with my thumb. "Yeah, something like that. Hey, Beck? If we're ever separated, I think it's important to have a meeting place."

"Wait? Why would we ever be sep . . . Oh." Beck laid back down on my lap, looking at her ring.

"May seventh. Every single May seventh at the New River Bridge. If we find ourselves starting over, I want you to meet me there as soon as you can," I said, stressing the importance.

"May seventh, the New River Bridge," Beck repeated. Reassurance washed over me like a warm blanket, and Beck and I took a deep breath in unison. She looked back up to the sky and reached her hand out in front of her as I stroked her hair. At first, I thought she was admiring her ring, but then I saw her pinching at the open air. Her eyes green and wondrous, she looked in between her fingers, perplexed. "Hey, Easton?"

"Huh?"

"What are these?" She tried to catch another but came up short.

I chuckled and marveled at her as she saw what love looked like for the first time. "It's love, Beck."

"It's . . . magical," she whispered.

CHAPTER 25

Neither one of us was ready for reality. We remained in the clearing above the Truly River for hours. Beck asked questions about her cancer, and I helped fill in the missing gaps in her memory. She told me stories she'd read in her journals and picked flower petals until the sun made its voyage across the sky.

When it was time to head back to reality, Beck and I strolled hand in hand on the trail under the pines. Beck tossed me the keys from her bag and I unlocked the car before we got inside. I pulled my seatbelt across my chest and noticed that Beck sat still and silent. She paged through her phone, which was filled with missed calls and texts. Several were undoubtedly from me, and I became insecure when Beck twisted with unease.

"What? I was worried, you weren't answering."

"It's from Nolan. James was in an accident!" Beck said in shock. I looked away, feeling her hot gaze on me, but I was too cowardly to meet her stare. I swallowed, feeling the push and pull of bad news on a beautiful day, and I put my car into reverse and pulled out of the pines. "He's at the St. Peterson Mercy Hospital. Do you know how to get there?" Beck asked. I did, it was the same hospital that Beck had been taken to by ambulance after her brother's wedding. I nodded, and we were in for a shift in the tide.

Beck stayed on phone calls between Nolan, Payton, and Brooklyn, and by the time we pulled into the hospital, there was a small group of James's close friends huddled in the waiting room. The few I knew were from our trip to Sin City, but there were several faces I'd never seen before. Beck ran into Brooklyn's arms, and I wondered if she'd had a dream about James, too. I took a seat, resting my elbows on my knees and hanging my head, my hair flopping into my face. The dread spread throughout my chest as I waited for news that only I could know to spread to his friends.

It was a scene I'd seen a few times too many and one I had never wanted to see again. It's hard enough to watch someone leave this world of old age—a perfectly natural occurrence that happens every single second—but when a person is young, short-changed, and unready . . . it's even more unfathomable. I wanted to be anywhere but in that waiting room, but I had a job, a love, and a breaking heart to protect.

James's friends talked amongst themselves as we waited for answers, and I gathered the bits of information that I could and pasted them together. From what I understood, James was on a job painting high on top of scaffolding when he tripped and fell. He landed in a compromising position and there was damage to his spinal cord and head.

He wasn't conscious when they brought him in, and I knew he was already gone, though monitors would most likely keep him alive for hours or even days longer. I watched his friends lean on each other, and when I saw no evidence of his parents, I asked Brooklyn where they were. "They're out of state on vacation. Nobody has got a hold of them yet," she said. I threw my head back and scratched my head, exasperated.

"I can't stay here. I need to walk. Tell Beck that I'll be right back, OK?" I asked.

"Absolutely. Oh, and Easton?" Brooklyn said. I looked over my shoulder as Brooklyn mouthed, "Congratulations," with an empathetic smile. I patted my heart and turned away. It was hard to be happy in the wake of a tragedy.

I fled the scene and made my way to the cafeteria for a coffee. Unbeknownst to me, Beck had followed. "Can I get a coffee please?" I asked.

"Just one?"

I looked behind me, startled to see Beck. "Two please," she said.

"Hey, I'm sorry, I just needed a breather," I apologized.

"I get it." Beck gripped my arm tight and rested her head on my shoulder, exhausted from an emotional couple of days. We took our coffees and headed to a nearby table littered with creamer and sugar packets. It was when Beck took her lid off, that I saw her mother enter the cafeteria. As quickly as I could, I spun Beck around, shielding the visibility of her face.

"Ah! What'd you do that for?" Beck held her arms up,

covered in hot coffee. Beck's mom looked towards us to see what the commotion was about, and I ducked my head.

"Shhh, wait!" I hissed.

Beck slapped her hand down on her thigh, "Easton, I'm covered in coffee!"

"Beck, it's your mom. She's here!" I whispered into Beck's ear.

Beck turned around slowly and I grabbed her wrist, leading her out of the cafeteria. Both of our coffees remained behind. Once in the safety of a stairwell, Beck looked into my eyes with an unwavering sense of knowing. "It's my dad, Easton. I just know it. I have to see him."

"Beck, we can't interfere. They won't understand," I pled.

"I'm not asking permission, Easton! I'm doing this with or without you, I'm only asking for your help!" Beck didn't wait for my answer and spun on her heels, ready to charge out of the stairwell.

"I can find him," I said, and Beck stopped. "This way," I said.

Together, we checked with a nurse. I told her I was Beck's brother, Carter, and she pointed us in her father's direction without a second thought. Beck squeezed my hand as we walked down the halls looking for her dad's room. When we found it, she took a moment to gather herself before entering.

Beck's dad lay resting while monitors captured his vitals. A clear breathing tube was threaded above his ears and under his nose, and his bedsheets were folded pristinely across his chest. The past twenty-one years had not been kind to him, and the broken heart of losing his daughter had shone in the crevices etched into his forehead.

"Pop?" Beck whispered.

"Shhh, we can't wake him," I said.

Beck pulled a seat near his bedside and sat down. Her face compressed with heavy emotion. I stood by the doorway keeping an eye out for her mother, and when I was convinced that we had some time alone, I picked up her dad's chart and read. Beck reached for her father's hand, causing my heart to skip a beat, but I couldn't tell her not to. Not just because she wouldn't listen but because the fear of her parents seeing her was far less than the fear of Beck not saying goodbye. In all honesty, had I been given the chance, I would risk it too.

She brought his hand to her lips and kissed his knuckles. Gentle tears rolled off her cheeks and dripped onto her lap. I watched as she finally had the chance to say goodbye to her dad, even if it was an entire lifetime late. I couldn't pry my eyes off of them, and I felt my own tears burning the corners of my eyes.

"I'm sorry I didn't get a chance to say goodbye, Pop. I thought I had more time. I thought it was going to be different," Beck murmured, lowering her head. Broken.

The corners of her dad's lips pulled up in a strained smile, and his eyes fluttered open. My stomach dropped and while I felt adrenaline course through my veins, Beck was the polar opposite. She remained calm and complacent. Confident that she was right where she ought to be.

"Everly? Everly, is that you?" he said through the drugs and heavy eyelids.

"It's me, Dad, I'm here. I'm here." Beck kissed his hand repeatedly, squeezing it tight.

"Oh, Beck! Oh, Beck. How I've missed you." He began to cry, his body brittle and quaking.

"Don't cry, Dad. I'm doing good. I'm happy, and I have Easton. He's taking care of me, so you don't need to worry about me anymore." Beck's dad looked at me, and his eyes grew wide. It hurt me to see his wounds reopening, and I wished it didn't have to be this way. I ran my hands through my hair and scanned the halls once more as my heart nearly lurched out of my chest in anticipation of what would come next.

"What's it like, Beck? What's it going to be like?"

Beck looked at me, taken aback by his question. My mouth fell open.

"Um . . ." Beck looked back to her father, her leg bouncing nervously. She exhaled long and methodically, collecting an answer that she would never know to be true. "It's like kicking your shoes off after a long day's work. It's like birds flying over a pond on a warm afternoon at sunset. It's um . . . it's football and a cold beer . . ." Beck's voice strained, barely audible anymore.

"Will you be there, Beck?" His eyes filled with tears.

"Yeah, Dad. I'll be there . . ." Beck pushed his white hair off of his forehead and ran the back of her hand down the side of his face.

"Listen, Dad. I can't stay. I have to go, but um . . . can you tell Mom something for me?"

Beck's dad covered his face, trying to stifle his sobs.

"Tell Mom that I borrowed my journals, but that I will give them back soon, OK? I don't want her to worry she failed me by losing them. It was me. I took them. And Dad, tell her I love her. Carter too." Beck stood to hug her dad goodbye.

When he pried his incredulous eyes off of her and placed them onto me, I walked over to him and leaned in close to his ear. "Sir, thank you for raising such an amazing daughter. You don't have to worry about her. I'll keep her safe. I promise," I said.

Beck buried her face into her sleeves, wiping away her tears. "Take care of my daughter," her dad said through a splintered voice, and I forced a smile and nodded.

"I will."

Beck looked to her dad when I joined her side and she whispered, "I love you, Pop."

He nodded, burying his eyes deep into his palms, sobbing even heavier yet. "I love you. I love you," he cried.

I looked to Beck, "We should go," I said. She nodded in agreement right as the footsteps approached the door. I panicked and pulled Beck behind the privacy curtain of the shared patient room. Beck's eyes were large with shock, but wider yet when we heard her mother's voice on the other side of the thin vale.

"Oh, honey, I'm here. What's wrong?"

"B . . . Beck . . . Beck" her dad murmured.

Beck cupped her mouth with both hands, trying to

silence her cry. Her tears ran down her cheeks and onto her interlocking fingers. I rubbed her back, trying desperately to keep her calm. The damage we had done was sinking in, and it would only be made worse if we showed ourselves now. My own heartbeat became deafening, and for a moment, it was the only thing that I could hear. That was until code blue was called.

Panic ensued on the other side of the curtain, nurses yelling, instruments clamoring. Above all was the screaming from his beloved. Beck began to hyperventilate, and I sat her down on the empty hospital bed as I blocked out the trauma as best I could by placing my hands over her ears. I fought to get her attention, which was no effortless task. When I had her eyes locked onto mine, I worked even harder to keep them there. We took deep breaths together, and I held her hands tight. As tight as I could.

"Clear!" a nurse yelled, and a thump sounded shortly thereafter. Beck and I held our breath until a tiny beep sounded for the second time. "We have a heartbeat! Let's get him to surgery now!"

Beck jumped off of the bed, weak at the knees. I stabled her trembling body in my embrace, and we listened to the commotion leave the room and trail down the halls. The curtain steadied in the wake of the storm. Only the feeble weeping of Beck's mother was left on the other side. So close, yet . . . still a lifetime away.

Beck had called the hospital that night for an update on her father, and when she got the news that he didn't make it, she started checking the newspaper for funeral updates. James hadn't made it either, and Beck was having a difficult time processing it all. She said it was easier when it was herself that was dying and that she would take their place if she could. She didn't understand why she couldn't. Why she got a second chance when they only had one shot.

Beck stayed at my house every night, and every day we moved in more boxes of her things. The once fixer-upper was fast becoming our home . . . my favorite place to be. Brooklyn gushed over Beck's ring and was happy to help her pack in the short stints that Beck spent at their apartment. Brooklyn even spent some time over at our house, and she quickly became a friend of mine as well. She promised to help Beck plan the wedding, and I relinquished all rights to any opinions I might have.

The following week ended with not one but two funerals. James's service was packed with new and old friends, co-workers, fellow students, and family. Brooklyn held Beck's hand at the burial and she often spun her engagement ring mindlessly. When the crowd thinned, Brooklyn's empty stare turned to me as she asked if I could fetch her jacket from her car. I welcomed the chance to step away for a breath of fresh air, though the heavy heart would follow. I strolled down the dirt path a little slower than usual as I played with her keys in my hand. I rummaged through multiple garments in Brooklyn's car before settling on the only one fancy enough to go with her dress. Passing James's friends on my way back to the grave,

Brooklyn had her arms wrapped around Beck as she stroked her hair. "Is she alright?" I asked, approaching.

"Just a little shaken up is all," Brooklyn said. I handed her the jacket from the car, and she let go of Beck to put it on. Beck's eyes flicked to me before turning back to Brooklyn. She gave her a quick nod before asking me if we could go home. Beck was silent, overcome with emotion, and by the next day at her father's funeral, she had said that she was numb. Hollow from the inside out.

The sun was high as we sat on a hilltop bench across the cemetery. Beck wore a large sunhat and matching black sunglasses. She could have passed for a celebrity in her mysterious way. There was a smaller gathering for her father, but that was to be expected at his age. Beck pointed out past relatives as she remembered them, and I pointed out her new niece that I had seen at The Taste of Italy. When the crowd dispersed after the burial, Beck's immediate family stayed behind, throwing flowers into the hole where her father's casket was lowered.

"Everly? Can you watch Wes? I don't want him to fall," Chloe said, pointing to the little boy. Beck's niece scooped up her little brother and bopped a white rose on his nose. We watched as he squealed trying to capture it. I squeezed Beck's hand, and a rogue tear tumbled down her cheek from behind her sunglasses, finding its way into the crevice of her lips.

"Is it always going to be like this?" Beck asked.

I thought about how many people I'd held at arm's length. How many people I'd distanced myself from so that

I could protect myself from this very moment. I had been doing it wrong all along. "If we're lucky," I said.

Beck's face was shielded by the brim of her black hat, but I could see her red lips twitch with disapproval. "How could you ever associate this feeling with luck?" Beck asked, as she stared down the hill at her family as an outsider.

I took a deep breath. I had been thinking about it a lot lately. "Because it means you're doing it right. You couldn't possibly hurt like this if you haven't loved like that," I said.

Beck let out a small sound that caught in her throat, and she pulled her hand away to wipe her cheek. It was then that a beautiful amethyst dragonfly fluttered up to Beck, landing on the lilac peonies she held for her father. I smiled and looked to Beck to see her lips press together before she lifted her hand to cup her mouth.

"Wow, Beck. It's really something, huh?"

Beck pulled her sunglasses down the bridge of her nose and peered at the dragonfly. A tender smile breached her lips, and I knew in that moment the stars had aligned just perfectly for us. I didn't know how or why. But I knew I had finally found my forever within her gentle soul.

"You know what my dad always used to say?" Beck asked as the purple dragonfly took flight.

"What's that?" I asked, watching it flutter to meet her family below. My heart warmed when I saw Beck's nephew take notice, chasing it around the grave site. Not a care in the world.

"When one door closes, another one opens . . ."

THANK YOU

Thank you for reading The Second Life of Everly Beck. If you enjoyed this story, please consider leaving a quick review or star rating. It makes my day.

ABOUT THE AUTHOR

Laura C. Reden is an emerging romance author who likes to add paranormal and fantasy twists while tugging at the heart strings.

Overcoming the struggles of dyslexia, Laura found that creative passion and hard work triumphs over her disadvantage.

Laura is a Southern Californian native, wife, and mother of two daughters. Her pastimes include video production, pottery, and horseback riding. While she received an education in social and behavioral science, she currently works as the chief financial officer for her family-owned law firm in San Diego.

If you are interested in staying updated on new releases, subscribe to my monthly email list. It's short and sweet with opportunities to help name characters, get advanced review copies, and even have your pet featured in upcoming scenes.

https://www.subscribepage.com/redenbooks

Xoxo,

Laura

ALSO BY

YOU'VE HEARD THE TERM «OLD SOUL» BEFORE,
BUT WHAT IF SOME SOULS NEVER REALLY DIE?

THE TETHERED SOUL SERIES

FOLLOW THE TRAGIC TALE OF A DYING GIRL,
AND BOY WITH AN IMMORTAL SOUL.

LAURA C. REDEN

DREAMS ARE FICKLE, EMOTIONS ARE BOLD.

THE
PHANTOM SERIES

CAUGHT BETWEEN WORLDS,
KINSLEY WILDE CAN SEE THE DEAD,
MANIFEST HER DREAMS, AND CONJURE HER FEARS.

BOOK CLUB NOTES:

BOOK CLUB NOTES:

9 781954 587182